AFRICAN WRITERS SERIES
FOUNDING EDITOR Chinua Achebe

PETER ABRAHAMS
6 *Mine Boy*

CHINUA ACHEBE
1 *Things Fall Apart*
3 *No Longer at Ease*
16 *Arrow of God*
31 *A Man of the People*
100 *Girls at War**
120 *Beware Soul Brother†*

THOMAS AKARE
241 *The Slums*

T. M. ALUKO
11 *One Man, One Matchet*
30 *One Man, One Wife*
32 *Kinsman and Foreman*
70 *Chief, the Honourable Minister*
130 *His Worshipful Majesty*
242 *Wrong Ones in the Dock*

ELECHI AMADI
25 *The Concubine*
44 *The Great Ponds*
210 *The Slave*

I. N. C. ANIEBO
148 *The Anonymity of Sacrifice*
206 *The Journey Within*
253 *Of Wives, Talismans and the Dead**

KOFI ANYIDOHO
261 *A Harvest of Our Dreams†*

AYI KWEI ARMAH
43 *The Beautyful Ones Are Not Yet Born*
154 *Fragments*
155 *Why Are We So Blest?*
194 *The Healers*
218 *Two Thousand Seasons*

BEDIAKO ASARE
59 *Rebel*

KOFI AWOONOR
108 *This Earth, My Brother*
260 *Until the Morning After†*

MARIAMA BÂ
248 *So Long a Letter*

FRANCIS BEBEY
205 *The Ashanti Doll*

MONGO BETI
13 *Mission to Kala*
77 *King Lazarus*
88 *The Poor Christ of Bomba*
181 *Perpetua and the Habit of Unhappiness*
214 *Remember Ruben*

STEVE BIKO
217 *I Write What I Like §*

OKOT P'BITEK
147 *The Horn of My Love†*
193 *Hare and Hornbill**
266 *Song of Lawino & Song of Ocol†*

YAW M. BOATENG
186 *The Return*

Nov
*Shor
†Poet
‡Play
§Biog

DENNI
46 *L
115 *A
208 *Stubborn Hope*

AMILCAR CABRAL
198 *Unity and Struggle §*

SYL CHENEY-COKER
221 *The Graveyard Also Has Teeth†*

DRISS CHRAIBI
79 *Heirs to the Past*

J. P. CLARK
50 *America, Their America §*

WILLIAM CONTON
12 *The African*

BERNARD B. DADIE
87 *Climbié*

DANIACHEW WORKU
125 *The Thirteenth Sun*

MODIKWE DIKOBE
124 *The Marabi Dance*

MBELLA SONNE DIPOKO
57 *Because of Women*
107 *Black and White in Love†*

AMU DJOLETO
41 *The Strange Man*

T. OBINKARAM ECHEWA
168 *The Land's Lord*

CYPRIAN EKWENSI
2 *Burning Grass*
5 *People of the City*
19 *Lokotown**
84 *Beautiful Feathers*
146 *Jagua Nana*
172 *Restless City**
185 *Survive the Peace*

BUCHI EMECHETA
227 *The Joys of Motherhood*

OLAUDAH EQUIANO
10 *Equiano's Travels §*

NURUDDIN FARAH
80 *From a Crooked Rib*
184 *A Naked Needle*
226 *Sweet and Sour Milk*
252 *Sardines*

MUGO GATHERU
20 *Child of Two Worlds §*

FATHY GHANEM
223 *The Man Who Lost His Shadow*

NADINE GORDIMER
177 *Some Monday for Sure**

JOE DE GRAFT
166 *Beneath the Jazz and Brass†*
264 *Muntu‡*

YUSUF IDRIS
209 *The Cheapest Nights**
267 *Rings of Burnished Brass**

OBOTUNDE IJIMERE
18 *The Imprisonment of Obatala‡*

EDDIE IROH
189 *Forty-Eight Guns for the General*
213 *Toads of War*
255 *The Siren in the Night*

KENJO JUMBAM
231 *The White Man of God*

AUBREY KACHINGWE
24 *No Easy Task*

SAMUEL KAHIGA
158 *The Girl from Abroad*

CHEIKH HAMIDOU KANE
119 *Ambiguous Adventure*

KENNETH KAUNDA
4 *Zambia Shall Be Free §*

LEGSON KAYIRA
162 *The Detainee*

A. W. KAYPER-MENSAH
157 *The Drummer in Our Time†*

JOMO KENYATTA
219 *Facing Mount Kenya §*

ASARE KONADU
40 *A Woman in her Prime*
55 *Ordained by the Oracle*

AHMADOU KOUROUMA
239 *The Suns of Independence*

MAZISI KUNENE
211 *Emperor Shaka the Great†*
234 *Anthem of the Decades†*
235 *The Ancestors†*

ALEX LA GUMA
35 *A Walk in the Night**
110 *In the Fog of the Seasons End*
212 *Time of the Butcherbird*

HUGH LEWIN
251 *Bandiet*

TABAN LO LIYONG
69 *Fixions**
74 *Eating Chiefs**
90 *Frantz Fanon's Uneven Ribs†*

YULISA AMADU MADDY
137 *No Past, No Present, No Future*

NAGUIB MAHFOUZ
225 *Children of Gebelawi*

NELSON MANDELA
123 *No Easy Walk to Freedom* §

JACK MAPANJE
236 *Of Chameleons and Gods* †

DAMBUDZO MARECHERA
207 *The House of Hunger* *
237 *Black Sunlight*

ALI A MAZRUI
97 *The Trial of Christopher Okigbo*

TOM MBOYA
81 *The Challenge of Nationhood (Speeches)* §

THOMAS MOFOLO
229 *Chaka*

DOMINIC MULAISHO
98 *The Tongue of the Dumb*
204 *The Smoke that Thunders*

JOHN MUNONYE
21 *The Only Son*
45 *Obi*
94 *Oil Man of Obange*
153 *A Dancer of Fortune*
195 *Bridge to a Wedding*

MARTHA MVUNGI
159 *Thee Solid Stones* *

MEJA MWANGI
143 *Kill Me Quick*
145 *Carcase for Hounds*
176 *Gang Down River Road*

GEORGE SIMEON MWASE
160 *Strike a Blow and Die* §

JOHN NAGENDA
262 *The Seasons of Thomas Tebo*

NGUGI WA THIONG O
7 *Weep Not Child*
17 *The River Between*
36 *A Grain of Wheat*
51 *The Black Hermit* ‡
150 *Secret Lives* *
188 *Petals of Blood*
200 *Devil on the Cross*
240 *Detained* §

NGUGI & MICERE MUGO
191 *The Trial of Dedan Kimathi* ‡

NGUGI & NGUGI WA MIRII
246 *I Will Marry When I Want* ‡

REBEKA NJAU
203 *Ripples in the Pool*

NKEM NWANKWO
67 *Danda*
173 *My Mercedes is Bigger Than Yours*

FLORA NWAPA
26 *Efuru*
56 *Idu*

S NYAMFUKUDZA
233 *The Non-Believer's Journey*

ONUORA NZEKWU
85 *Wand of Noble Wood*

OLUSEGUN OBASANJO
249 *My Commands* §

OGINGA ODINGA
38 *Not Yet Uhuru* §

GABRIEL OKARA
68 *The Voice*
183 *The Fisherman's Invocation* †

CHRISTOPHER OKIGBO
62 *Labyrinths* †

KOLE OMOTOSO
122 *The Combat*

SEMBENE OUSMANE
63 *God's Bits of Wood*
92 *The Money-Order*
175 *Xala*
250 *The Last of the Empire*

YAMBO OUOLOGUEM
99 *Bound to Violence*

FERDINANDO OYONO
29 *Houseboy*
39 *The Old Man and the Medal*

SOL T. PLAATJE
201 *Mhudi*

PEPETELA
269 *Mayombe*

R. L. PETENI
178 *Hill of Fools*

LENRIE PETERS
22 *The Second Round*
37 *Satellites* †
238 *Selected Poetry* †

MOLEFE PHETO
258 *And Night Fell* §

J. J. RABEARIVELO
167 *Translations from the Night* †

ALIFA RIFAAT
271 *Distant View of a Minaret*

MWANGI RUHENI
156 *The Minister's Daughter*

TAYEB SALIH
47 *The Wedding of Zein* *
66 *Season of Migration to the North*

STANLAKE SAMKANGE
33 *On Trial for my Country*
169 *The Mourned One*
190 *Year of the Uprising*

WILLIAMS SASSINE
199 *Wirriyamu*

KOBINA SEKYI
136 *The Blinkards* ‡

SAHLE SELLASSIE
163 *Warrior King*

FRANCIS SELORMEY
27 *The Narrow Path*

L. S. SENGHOR
71 *Nocturnes* †
180 *Prose and Poetry*

SIPHO SEPAMLA
268 *A Ride on the Whirlwind*

MONGANE SEROTE
263 *To Every Birth Its Blood*

WOLE SOYINKA
76 *The Interpreters*

TCHICAYA U TAM'SI
72 *Selected Poems* †

CAN THEMBA
104 *The Will to Die* *

REMS NNA UMEASIEGBU
61 *The Way We Lived* *

J. L. VIEIRA
202 *The Real Life of Domingos Xavier*
222 *Luuanda*

JOHN YA-OTTO
244 *Battlefront Namibia* §

ASIEDU YIRENKYI
216 *Kivuli and Other Plays* †

D. M. ZWELONKE
128 *Robben Island*

COLLECTIONS OF PROSE
9 *Modern African Prose*
14 *Quartet*
23 *The Origin of Life and Death*
48 *Not Even God is Ripe Enough*
83 *Myths and Legends of the Congo*
118 *Amadu's Bundle*
132 *Two Centuries of African English*
192 *Egyptian Short Stories*
243 *Africa South Contemporary Writings*
254 *Stories from Central and Southern Africa*
256 *Unwinding Threads*
259 *This is the Time*
270 *African Short Stories*

ANTHOLOGIES OF POETRY
8 *A Book of African Verse*
93 *A Choice of Flowers*
96 *Poems from East Africa*
106 *French African Verse*
129 *Igbo Traditional Verse*
164 *Black Poets in South Africa*
171 *Poems of Black Africa*
192 *Anthology of Swahili Poetry*
215 *Poems from Angola*
230 *Poets to the People*
257 *New Poetry from Africa*

COLLECTIONS OF PLAYS
28 *Short East African Plays*
34 *Ten One-Act Plays*
78 *Short African Plays*
127 *Nine African Plays for Radio*
165 *African Plays for Playing 1*
179 *African Plays for Playing 2*
224 *South African People's Plays*
232 *Egyptian One-Act Plays*

CYPRIAN EKWENSI

Beautiful Feathers

HEINEMANN
LONDON IBADAN NAIROBI

Heinemann Educational Books Ltd
22 Bedford Square, London WC1B 3HH
P.M.B. 5205 Ibadan · P.O. Box 45314 Nairobi

EDINBURGH MELBOURNE AUCKLAND
KINGSTON HONG KONG SINGAPORE NEW DELHI
KUALA LUMPUR

Heinemann Education Books Inc.
70 Court Street, Portsmouth, New Hampshire 03801, USA

ISBN 0 435 90084 6

© Cyprian Ekwensi 1963
First published by Hutchinson 1963
First published in *African Writers* 1971
Reprinted 1975, 1977, 1978, 1982, 1986

Printed in Great Britain by
Richard Clay (The Chaucer Press) Ltd, Bungay, Suffolk

To
Leopold Sedar Senghor
of
Negritude Fame

and

Alhaji Sir Abubakar Tafawa Balewa
Patron,
Society of Nigerian Authors

Beautiful Feathers

'However famous a man is outside, if he is not respected inside his own home he is like a bird with *beautiful feathers*, wonderful on the outside but ordinary within.' So runs the Ibo proverb which provides the theme for Cyprian Ekwensi's new novel.

Wilson Iyari, the leader of the Nigerian Movement for African and Malagasy Solidarity, commands the respect of the masses. Among the leaders of African thought his name has significance. But inside his home he has no authority. He is disregarded, then deserted, by his own wife. While he pursues his desire for African and Malagasy Solidarity his home life is crumbling and he cannot concentrate on running his business: the INDEPENDENCE PHARMACY. Wilson does not come to terms with himself until he discovers that unity is a complex of the judicious and proper, the overlooked and forgotten, the tolerated and rejected. Like *Jagua Nana*, Cyprian Ekwensi's previous novel published by Hutchinson, *Beautiful Feathers* is highly entertaining and holds the reader's attention to the last page.

1

WHENEVER Wilson arrived at his pharmacy in the evenings there was always a small number of patients waiting to seek his advice, and quite often a few of them wanted something more than to have their prescriptions dispensed. As he drove behind the lorry he pictured the small group already assembled in his waiting-room, impatient, expectant. Even before he parked his car he saw one of them—a woman with a child strapped to her back—starting towards the road intent on intercepting him. He quickly swung his car in the direction of the shop and eased it to the foot of the telegraph pole where he usually parked it. To his annoyance a lorry was already parked there, unloading passengers. The suburban bus drivers had converted the front of his pharmacy into an improvised bus stop, and—true to their nickname *Bole-kaja* (get down, let's fight)—they always made sure there was a fight each time they stopped there.

He got out of his car, waded straight into baskets of leaves, tomatoes and gari, hurriedly tumbled down from the lorry. He was jostled by quarrelling women and heckled by the swearing collector. A big-bosomed woman shouldered him and he performed a compulsory hurdle over a bag of beans. He had neither the time nor the patience to spare for the fight which immediately flared up around him. The contestants were the woman and the collector. One glance told him that the big-bosomed woman had not a chance against the collector's brutality. She had seized him by the shirt and was screaming with all her might, something about change. The collector shoved her violently on her bosom and disengaged her grip. Amid cheers he leapt on to the tailboard of the wagon, which careered off to the accompaniment of the woman's yelling voice and obscenely pointing fingers. Wilson shook his head. One day he would take up this matter of the improvised bus stop with the Town Clerk.

It was the twilight hour now, when this suburb of Lagos is usually in something of a scramble. At the far corner of the street the girls from the Modern School were pouring into the street after their evening classes. One of the girls in her short white frock and blue belt smiled a high-heeled smile at him. Her lipstick was brighter than anything a mature woman would ever dare to use, and the make-up on her face could have plastered the end wall of a room. Wilson concluded that she must be one of the schoolgirls of modern Nigeria and he had to look hard and close to discover the loveliness beneath the paint. Though her eyes twinkled with recognition, he was sure he had never seen her before. Indeed, schoolgirls came to his pharmacy to ask for aphrodisiacs, contraceptives and abortifacients, depending on their state of charge and the time of the month; but this one was new to him.

She was making straight for him, still smiling. 'Excuse me, sah . . . Aren't you Wilson Iyari?'

He nodded and she said: 'I saw your picture in the paper. You are the new leader of the NMFAMS . . . I only want to salute you, sah, as leader of the Nigerian Movement for African and Malagasy Solidarity. . . . I am a secretary-typist in the Ministry of Consolation . . . My name is Chini.'

'A secretary-typist? But I thought . . .'

'My uniform?' She smiled. 'That's only because I attend evening classes. . . . I'm learning French. Every Tuesday evening, six to eight.'

'Chini. . . . I too have seen your face somewhere before.'

'In the papers,' she said. 'In the gossip column. You know what the journalists are like. I accompanied some Ministers on their world tours, you see. . . . And again, that scandal when my husband left me. . . . I want to forget it now.'

Wilson remembered her now. Chini Moka. Her husband had left her for a much older woman who was now proving childless. They shook hands, and as they talked Wilson felt immediately the sudden interest taken in their conversation by passers-by. From all sides of the street faces peered at them. By any standards Wilson Iyari was a man who would attract attention anywhere. He was light of skin, straight-nosed and tall. He wore white robes, a black cap and black court shoes. His father was an Eastern Nigerian, a Calabar man who had abandoned his mother—a fulani from Northern Nigeria—soon after Wilson began attending primary school. From both of them Wilson had inherited his light skin, but in addition he bore his father a grudge for shirking his responsibility by leaving him to battle his way through life. Even now, at thirty, he still looked at the world through grudging eyes dimmed with bitter memories of toil and loneliness, especially in his anxious days in London. In the few weeks since the crisis in the Nigerian Movement for African and Malagasy Solidarity, which had led to his being appointed the new leader, he had sprouted a beard which gave him a certain air of aggressiveness associated with the out-of-date Nationalists of the Colonial era. Yet he had a pleasant twinkle in his eye and the girls never seemed to ignore him.

Wilson felt a glow of pride as the girl talked to him there in the open bus stop with the traffic halting and heads peering out of car windows. He knew she was talking to him for the sheer distinction of standing in the open street with Wilson Iyari, leader of the Nigerian Movement for African and Malagasy Solidarity.

Her bus arrived and with a wave she hurried towards it. The lights were coming on in the streets as the bus tunnelled through the conglomeration of cyclists, taxis, pedestrians from the market and the schools. Wilson immediately cast Chini's image out of his mind. He was no longer shocked by the daily challenge of total strangers speaking familiarly with him: the petty traders on the Marina, the bus drivers, the élite, they all knew him and stopped to speak with him. It was good for the retail sales in the pharmacy. As a pharmacist he would have been known and respected. Many of his professional friends were. But Wilson Iyari was also the voice of the younger people of his generation, a man apart. Most of the time he thought about the NMFAMS, but in the evenings, as now, he came to the INDEPENDENCE PHARMACY and puzzled out the health problems of the city dwellers.

He opened the pharmacy door and the aroma of drugs struck his senses with a sharp welcome. His clients threw him welcoming smiles and words of appreciation. Their respect for his professional knowledge caressed and fondled him.

He sat down and felt a flood of satisfaction. It occurred to him that, unlike at home, here was one place in the world where he was appreciated. In the NMFAMS he was a man, a leader. On the streets people stopped to speak with him. But there remained his own home: and there he was nothing—a man without respect. He never admitted it to others, but in moments like this the revelation always saddened him.

In the waiting-room of the INDEPENDENCE PHARMACY the children were whimpering on their mothers' backs. The prescriptions lay in a stack. Wilson put down his brief-case, greeted his patients and swept the cards off the table. From the woman who had seemed so impatient he took a card and went into the dispensing section. The girl in the white overall smiled, but immediately tackled the work of mixing and compounding. Wilson stood by, checking the poisons and dangerous drugs, making entries into his books and generally supervising the mixing of the magic liquids that brought health to thousands. He thought: When African Solidarity is eventually achieved there will be hundreds of new pharmacies everywhere on the continent. There will be research schemes into African herbs, roots, barks . . . the results will be Africa's own contribution to medical science. At the moment pharmacy is waiting for Africa's contribution.

He came out with the bottles and boxes and tubes and phials. He distributed them, giving the bottle and the tablets to the impatient woman and himself going over the directions with her. She beamed her gratitude. She prayed that God lengthen his life. The child fixed big eyes on him. Wilson again felt an exaltation of his spirit.

In the interval his pharmacy had filled with young

men obviously not patients. He recognized them as members of the NMFAMS. Kwame Amantu, his deputy, was there. He shook their hands one by one and spoke to them. When the patients had cleared they told him that they had come to sound him on the proposed demonstration by the NMFAMS. Wilson shared their impatience but he also had his reservations. He pointed out the obvious limitations. *You don't just demonstrate. There must be a reason, valid or invalid. They would have to wait for some special event like the Independence Anniversary, but in the meantime they must hold themselves in readiness.*

The phone interrupted them. With pen and paper poised to take down some doctor's order, Wilson picked up the receiver. He heard instead the imperious voice of his wife.

'Willy, it's me—Yaniya.'

In the awkward pause, he thought: Well! Pursuing me even here!

'Is Brother Jacob there?' she asked.

Wilson looked round the waiting-room. Indeed, among the new arrivals was Brother Jacob, his wife's brother. His eager eyes now fixed themselves on Wilson's face.

'If he's there,' continued his wife, 'I want you to help him. You hear? That's all.' She rang off.

Wilson stared round the room. Rings like a target-board formed before his eyes. So it had reached this stage now. Yaniya giving him orders in his pharmacy. There was something vaguely sinister about it all. Quietly he replaced the receiver and turned to the boys. They were talking more loudly now about the coming demonstration, how they would march down from Yaba, across the bridge and into Lagos Island, carrying placards on the theme of African Solidarity. They would invite support from all the African Heads of Independent States and from the major African universities. Some of them held that there was no need to wait for a special event before staging the demonstration. One of them argued that the subject of African Solidarity was always there, the burden of Independence.

During the discussion Wilson noticed in the corner of the room Brother Jacob trying to catch his eye. There was no avoiding him now. He came up to Wilson and said, 'Can I see you a moment?'

He had sat tense throughout the discussion, contributing nothing. In the NMFAMS they knew him as a man who could assemble masses of people quickly and effectively. He could convert three votes to a thousand—for a consideration.

Wilson stepped with him into the corridor. Brother Jacob came straight to the point. 'I'm down,' he said. He looked Wilson straight in the eye. 'Raise me.'

Wilson stared back at him. Brother Jacob returned his stare without embarrassment. He lit a cigarette, drew on it and knitted his brows. He was impeccably dressed in a white jumper, white trousers with narrow bottoms and a black fez cap with the gold crest of the NMFAMS. There was a perpetual drunken stare in his eye, but years of living in the city had polished his movements to an irritating state of sophistication, so that he had become one big deceit.

'Business is bad, my dear in-law!'

Wilson felt the anger rising in him. 'Business . . . bad? Which business?' He had already foreseen the impending demand for a loan, never to be repaid.

Brother Jacob did not smile. 'Everything. . . . It's a bad time for everybody, very bad. . . . I have just been talking with the Minister about the contract for the Corporation. D'you know . . . Oh, no need to go into details. . . .'

Wilson knew Brother Jacob. His schemes were as grandiose as they were incredible. Wilson envied him the way his lies kept him in good supply of glamorous fat-bottomed girls and devoted hangers-on. Brother Jacob's business involved big names and easy money. Wilson heard stories but he was yet to see any concrete proof. He had heard Brother Jacob talk of the disposal of land which he did not possess. He had seen him produce an impressive map of the undeveloped land area of the city and heard him elaborate on the Government's future plans. Brother Jacob seemed to know all the newly completed flats and claimed that the sub-letting of the flats (five years' rent in advance) lay in his power. Wilson had heard that he was able to obtain driving licences for those who had taken no tests, to secure Government contracts for firms that had never sent in a tender. Brother Jacob was said to 'fix' jobs for new school-leavers who had left their school certificates behind. At election time he arranged for voters to support the candidate who had made him most comfortable. It was in this capacity that Wilson felt he would be most useful when the demonstration time came.

Round the clock, Brother Jacob was apparently well occupied. He knew the Chief of Police and was in turn known by the most insignificant corporal. He was always neatly dressed, chain-smoking and driving a car (unlicensed), so Wilson concluded he must be prospering. Yet he would come up to him for a loan of a few pounds. He was 'down' now, and only money could 'raise' him. It was clear to Wilson now why his wife had phoned. Brother Jacob must have called at the house soon after he left.

'I want you to help him!' she had commanded. He and Yaniya were not on speaking terms otherwise.

Brother Jacob was talking. '. . . and I'm hoping to get one per cent of that. Only one million pounds contract this time. Mind you, they're trying to cut it down. But I've advised the Minister against it. But, in-law, I'm only asking for a mere fifty pounds. It's not something I'll not refund.'

Wilson looked at him sharply. It was not the first time Jacob had promised to 'refund' without ever intending to keep his promise. Wilson as an 'in-law' was not expected to remind him too pointedly. He was tempted now to be firm in his refusal, but again he remembered Yaniya's voice on the telephone. 'I want you to help him.' The first thing she would want to know when he got home was whether Brother Jacob had called and what he had done for him. But what did he want fifty pounds for? Merely to squander?

'I'm only a pharmacist, you know,' Wilson said lamely, 'not a Minister. You are used to dealing with Ministers. Fifty pounds to me is a lot of money. Again, it is not my money but the money of the INDEPENDENCE PHARMACY. I have to account for every penny of it to the company.'

The words sounded vague and flat. Brother Jacob waved his signet-ring and smiled. He was talking without a pause.

Wilson thought fast. That afternoon, as was his custom since he had been robbed, he had transferred most of his takings to the bank. There would not be much money now in the cash register.

He went into the retail shop and took out the pound notes left. 'Only fourteen here,' he said, handing them over to Jacob.

Jacob thumbed through them with a contemptuous leer.

Wilson said: 'It's better than nothing. And, after all, the night is still young.'

'You mean...? No, I'm not going elsewhere to borrow money. What you can do is sufficient for me.' He drew at his cigarette and puffed it at the ceiling. 'Listen to me, in-law. I told you I'm down. You're my in-law and you can't be here while I go around the town begging everybody I see for money. I've got some pride. You know that. Oh yes!' His eyes glinted.

'Let's see what tomorrow will bring,' Wilson said.

Brother Jacob patted Wilson on the shoulder. Wilson drew away at the familiarity. Brother Jacob said: 'What you said just now is quite true.... I mean what you said to those boys in the room about the demonstration.' He looked over his shoulder and lowered his voice. 'I agree with you. We must have a reason. We can't just demonstrate like babies. We're grown-ups. I'm arranging to bring down people from Jos, Oyo, Port Harcourt. We want a big show, an All-Nigeria demonstration. Oh yes! No joke!'

Wilson beamed. 'The Nigerian Movement for African and Malagasy Solidarity will set the example for all Africa.'

'Have you got a reply yet to the letter you sent to the secretary of the Pan Africa Movement?'

'Not yet,' said Wilson.

'I know they'll accept. You work on and be patient.' He shrugged his shoulders and changed the subject. 'How's your wife?'

'What? You mean—your sister Yaniya? She's all right.'

'She's not being difficult?' Brother Jacob asked, in the protective voice of an in-law.

'No, no! . . . We're quite happy.'

'Good! In-law, you know . . . you have to be patient with women.' He knitted his brow. 'I know my own sister and she's a good girl. A very good girl. When she was a little girl our father spoilt her, you see. Gave her everything she asked. Of course, as a princess, what would you expect? And she was the youngest, and we the elder brothers and sisters again spoilt her more. But, you know, times have changed. You have to bear with her. She's wayward, but, Wilson, you have a very loyal wife. Very loyal. Oh, you should see how she stands up for you when anyone tries to talk ill of you. That's what I call loyalty. Oh yes!' He paused, then added: 'Bear with her. If she does anything wrong just have some patience. I know your task is hard. You are running this pharmacy, you are trying to bring about the unity of African States through the NMFAMS. But, you see, women never understand. That's why you must have patience. Oh yes. Yaniya is not a bad girl.'

He raised his black fez cap, smiled and slipped out into the streets. Wilson smiled back indulgently. Matrimonial advice from Brother Jacob. For all his wisdom he had never married. He had kept women, had lived with them in fleeting moments of prosperity, but he had no wife. Brother Jacob was standing at the improvised bus stop, watching the taxis speed by. He looked left, then right and raised his arm. A green-and-yellow taxi drew up and he took it and disappeared into the city with Wilson's fourteen pounds in his pockets.

Wilson went back to the impromptu meeting of the NMFAMS in his waiting-room, but for him the evening was really at an end.

2

He was thinking about the NMFAMS as he drove back home. His little boy, Lumumba, ran into the street crying: 'Papa, Papa, you done come back? You done return? Somebody come here to look for you. He carry motor come. He wear fine dress.'

Lumumba was Wilson's first-born son by Yaniya. Wilson loved him because he was his heir and spoilt him because he was the first. Since the African and Malagasy States began their emergence, Wilson had suddenly conceived the idea of re-naming all his children by the names of leading Nationalists. Little Lumumba embraced him, clinging about his legs. He took his father's brief-case away, asking in English: 'What you buy, Papa? You buy sweet? Why you no buy sweet? Why you no buy ice-cream?' He pulled at the catch. Wilson had forgotten to buy either sweets or ice-cream.

To his little mind whenever Papa went out it was to buy sweets or ice-cream, or coconut. Little Lumumba cared nothing about the NMFAMS or the INDEPENDENCE PHARMACY. He had been to the pharmacy a number of times and it always frightened him. Lumumba said, 'I no will play you again.' He flung aside the brief-case. 'I never will play you again!'

Wilson took him by the shoulder and whispered

promises. His two other children had seen him now and began beating their wings and opening their gums with pleasure. Wilson cooed at this one, patted that one. Pandhit, the young girl, stretched out her elegant hand. At two she was beautiful. Jomo, the smallest, sat complacent in a push-chair, beamed lazily and made some futile efforts to disengage himself. He was only twelve months old and thoroughly disliked any form of physical exercise. He hated sitting, crawling, walking. At twelve months, when all the children in his age group could be seen running around, he had only just begun to crawl, which everyone said was very slow for a child born to the African sunshine. They said the girls were quicker and it was true that Pandhit was walking in nine months.

His wife sat like a frozen stone, her face long, angry, resentful, indifferent. Looking at her face, Wilson experienced a chilly feeling. He could hardly mumble a greeting at her. She heard it, but stared coldly ahead. He went into his room, took off his clothes. When he came out in shirt and wrapper she was still sitting where she was, with no visible effort to welcome him. He called the houseboy, who told him that Madam had not ordered that any food be prepared for him. He was angry. It was now three days since Yaniya had prepared a meal of any kind for him, and he hated hotel food.

To divert his own mind from any thoughts of violence or angry action, he turned to his papers on the Nigerian Movement and read through them. But he could not concentrate on the facts and he went into the kitchen and put on a kettle. The houseboy would not allow him to do any work. He was 'Masta', leader of the NMFAMS. Very soon the boy had some food served on the table while Yaniya sat by, glum as ever.

Wilson saw the look of awe on Little Lumumba's face. Pandhit and the boy had gathered in a frightened group round their mother. They always knew when all was not well in the house. Wilson hated this atmosphere. He thought: *Solidarity, where does it begin? Here, in my own home? I am the leader of the Nigerian Movement for African and Malagasy Solidarity. Wilson Iyari, good looking, famous outside. At home I am nothing. I am like a fowl with beautiful feathers on the outside for all to see. When the feathers are removed the flesh and bones underneath are the same as for any other fowl. I am not really different from other men. In fact, if only they knew how I am spited in my own home they would despise me. They would never again listen to me talking about solidarity.*

He did not talk after his meal but began reading the text of a lecture by Zik on Pan Africanism. Whenever he began to lose himself in his books Yaniya immediately felt neglected.

'Why did Brother Jacob come and see you?'

Wilson went on reading.

'You helped him?' she said.

Nothing annoyed him more than this arrogance. She was in need, her whole family was in need, but she would always want to make it look as if she were bestowing a favour by accepting help. He turned over a page, and without lifting his face said: 'I did what I could. He asked for fifty pounds. I gave him fourteen. It was all the money left in the cash register.' Why did he have to defend his action? He kept his face down.

'Fourteen pounds out of fifty! Ridiculous!' He knew that note of mockery. This was the note that told him he was a loafer, a no-good, a failure, a poor stingy pharmacist, a man of no estate. It angered him. 'You help everyone, but when it comes to my own brother, your in-law, you have no money. You have enough money for your girls outside. Those riff-raffs in your party——'

Wilson put aside the papers. 'I will not have you call the boys riff-raffs. If you do not understand what the NMFAMS stands for you can at least keep quiet!' The words hurt him as they hurtled out. But he had to take a firm stand. He was surprised to find that they had no effect on her.

'One day you will all be locked up,' she said, and got up.

She was gorgeous. She took little Jomo on her shoulders. Pandhit clung to her wrapper and they all went into the room, a little clique around their mother. Wilson was jealous. Only Little Lumumba lingered behind. He hesitated, then came and sat by his father, who began stroking his hair.

'I am not running that shop for a joke,' Wilson muttered, after his wife. 'What guarantee have I that I shall ever see my fourteen pounds again? And if it had been fifty! And what did he want the money for, anyway? These wretched in-laws! What is the future of the INDEPENDENCE PHARMACY if I clear my cash-box any evening your brother cares to walk into the shop, stinking of whisky? And tomorrow you will be the first to laugh at me and call me a poor man, a failure; you will compare me with the other boys who are now Ministers and you will say I am a man of no estate!'

From her bedroom she was hurling angry words back at him. Her voice jarred on his senses. Then he heard her sobbing loudly and the children joined in chorus with her.

Wilson held his little son and said to him: 'When you grow up pray you do not marry one such as her. She is glamorous, and good fun as a girl friend. Oh yes. But she has never heard about the duties of a wife. Don't tell me I did not see something in her before I married her. . . . But what has really happened? Why has the whole thing become so unbearable since I became leader of the NMFAMS? Yes, I can trace it back to that time. Yaniya has become like an enemy inside my own house since I became leader of the NMFAMS.'

The boy looked at him, his eyes wide open, not understanding.

3

When Wilson first met her, Yaniya was a glamorous young woman of nineteen, tall, hard-breasted and elegant, with a face sculptured out of Benin Bronzes, and descended directly from the famous Emotan whose statue dominates the city of Benin. Iyari was then a Government pharmacist, working from eight in the morning to two in the afternoon. Life was not unduly hectic, and she had all his attention.

She had come to the hospital pharmacy that afternoon, sent by the doctor on emergency duty, to collect some serum, but as the chief pharmacist had gone home with the key to the refrigerator, she had to wait until the messenger went to his home to fetch it. Wilson gave her a seat inside the pharmacy. The crowd outside his window milled and pressed and protested, reminding him that patients were not allowed inside the pharmacy. He tossed aside their cards.

Something about this girl's personality impressed itself unforgettably on Wilson's mind. He sensed immediately that she had breeding, beauty and elegance. Her hair was striking and distinctive, piled high above her head and secured at the nape of the neck with a glittering pin. It was not raining, but she carried a slim umbrella and her dress was cut in two pieces of a light material, cool to the eyes and carefully matched with everything she wore.

Her skirt was drawn up tight about her knees, displaying smooth-skinned legs and beautiful feet. Her left leg bore the only mark of ugliness visible: the tooth-marks of a dog. Yaniya was supple, female and independent. She sat quiet but courteous till the key arrived, and within him was growing a proud possessiveness, shutting away the noisy chatter at the pharmacy window. When she had left he looked at his hands. The palms were wet with sweat. They were always that way when he was excited.

He did not meet her again until much later—at a christening party on Lewis Street. It was one of those parties held under improvised palm-frond shelters. The people of Lagos screen off one end of a street. Chairs built from light wood are placed in rows. People overflow into the thoroughfare and the traffic has to be diverted by the police. On this occasion Wilson stood admiring the powerful electric bulbs shining on to the light-blue blouses worn by the women: all of them in the same light-blue blouse, each with a large hibiscus flower embroidered on the breast. He saw Yaniya executing a slow, hip-rolling dance, and as she lifted her face his heart missed a beat. Her mouth opened in sudden recognition. She had come with an escort and he could not speak with her as long as he wished, but he managed to arrange a meeting. It was to be the first of many.

They began to meet more frequently and once she came to his pharmacy during her lunch period. After that he was transferred to the Orthopaedic Hospital in another part of the city, and from there to the Maternity Hospital. They began eating their lunch together at the Zapataya, and in the evenings they would go dancing or to the pictures. At week-ends she came and lived with him, cooking all his meals, polishing and scrubbing his two-roomed flatlet.

It was very much a Lagos courtship. Their parents were too far away to interfere. No one was present to ask questions about who slept where or with whom; Wilson did not seriously think of marrying her. But one morning he went to the hospital and they handed him an official letter. He was to proceed on transfer in fourteen days' time. Casually, he showed the note to Yaniya during the lunch break. She broke into tears. She vowed that if Wilson left her she would kill herself. In the evening her eyes were still swollen and the next day it was the same. The brightness had gone out of her life. She neglected her looks. Grief-stricken, she stared about her absently. He was confounded. Never could he once imagine that she had put her whole soul into the affair. He began to look at her with new eyes.

Yaniya had come to Lagos from Benin in search of work, and against her father's wish she had stayed on. She had not found it easy and, being beautiful, the men had wolfed her and left her heart-broken and faithless. One child was the direct result and after his death she again became pregnant. An abortion followed which nearly killed her. She was determined to have no more men in her life, to live strictly and to work and earn just enough to pay her rent and buy herself clothes. Men had tested her, but they had been repulsed and had come to the conclusion that one so beautiful must be abnormal in some manner. She would have continued her celibate life, but Wilson's kindness had again opened her heart.

Wilson suggested she ask for leave of absence and come with him to his new station. At the department store, where she worked as a floor supervisor, she was not due to go on leave for another eight months. The management refused to grant her either leave or transfer. Wilson tried to nullify his own transfer so he could remain at headquarters in Lagos, near Yaniya. He failed. The medical authorities reminded him that Nigeria was one country. He must serve wherever he was posted. That determined him. He would take Yaniya along with him.

They had been living together for about three weeks now. She had given up her single room, selling her furniture and coming over in a suitcase-laden taxi. Since then the spinsterly hollows (so often misnamed 'slimness') had vanished from her cheeks, which now filled with a new radiance. The eager male-hunt look in her eye was gone and in its place was a luminescent maturity nurtured by a love almost motherly. Yaniya was at the peak of her bloom. Wilson jocularly asked her, and she confessed: a baby was on the way. He decided immediately to marry her. She was overjoyed.

They had their honeymoon in Accra. Looking back on that fortnight in Ghana's *Avenida*, Wilson lingered with pleasure on the happiest time in their lives. He wished now that things could have remained just like that—full of dreams, brilliant with success. But as soon as they returned from Ghana, Wilson knew he must not continue much longer in the service of the Government. He must establish his own pharmacy, on however modest a scale. He told Yaniya all about his plans. In Nigeria there was always room for the good medical man, and if he drew on the field experience he already had in working with doctors in three different kinds of hospital, he was bound to succeed.

Yaniya wanted to contribute something to the well-being of the new family so they could build together. She decided on a course in dressmaking, something she could practise while keeping house. She proved so adept with the needle that the Institute begged her specially to remain with them as an instructress. The wage was good and her hours of work did not unduly conflict with her one keen desire at the time: to look after Wilson. It was her big dream then. She often told Wilson how she had been wolfed and swindled by Lagos men whose tongues were faster than their hired motor-cars, whose lies could always bed but never feed a woman. The dazzle had gone from her eyes and now the time had come to turn her back on her past life and build a new home. All this she revealed in her ardour. One day she would take Wilson to Benin, she promised. She would show him to her father, and say, 'Did you not say I would never find happiness in Lagos?' One day.

Wilson in his courtship days did not see how extravagant she was. He did not see her fanatical devotion to clothes, lipstick, mascara, rouge, nail varnish and all the false apparatus of deceit so flagrantly misused by initiates to the art of glamour. He heard her tinny laughter, and it excited him then. He saw her attachment to the ephemerals of the city—garden parties, dances, football matches, purposeless meetings.... To him at the time it was a symbol of her 'sociableness'. He knew she had lived much longer than he in the city, and therefore knew more men. She attracted them and at first he was disconcerted by the expensive robes he saw hanging from the railings of her bed. Not even her assurance that they belonged to her 'brother' satisfied him. Did her brother also own the different long cars that daily parked in front of her house?

In his love-blindness he had never once stopped to ask himself why those sleek Lagos men (who properly belonged to her set) did not marry her. Or could it be that marriage was not part of the game? Marriage must be something reserved for the slow-witted and he was too deeply in love to stop and calculate. Now there were three children and he could see things in a cold light. In his present position as leader of the Nigerian Movement for African and Malagasy Solidarity he could not afford to go through the scandal of a cleavage in his married life. Where did unity begin? He was sure she knew that, hence her new attitude. It would be a natural headline for a paper like the *West African Sensation*. The only way out of it all was to put up a placid front. He and Yaniya must still continue to be seen in public. They must smile and entertain, hold hands and say meaningless things for the benefit of the photographers and reporters, while underneath their hearts rotted with hate. This was the new Africa, deadly in its subtlety.

Soon after his first son Obi was born (they called him Obi then, but later changed his name to Little Lumumba), Wilson decided that it was time to break with the Government. He had completed his side of his scholarship contract, having served for three years after his training. He called his new pharmacy IYARI CHEMISTS (later he was to change the name to INDEPENDENCE PHARMACY in keeping with the times). The mild success of his enterprise brought the first flood of Yaniya's relatives with 'give me' hands outstretched. Their 'in-lawness' had become a one-sided affair in which they as bride-givers became perpetual recipients of gifts and support from the bride-taker. Wilson would have been only too glad to help them if Yaniya still loved him or showed the slightest sign of regard for him. He had often told her: You are the link. My in-laws are only important in relation to my happiness with you.

In those early days he could not exactly foresee his present predicament. At home he was happy. About him a restlessness was stirring in the African continent. He felt it. He heard how, one after another, African nations were breaking away from Colonial rule, splitting off to set up States on their own. Wilson had his early training in politics as branch secretary to the National Council of Nigeria and the Cameroons. One evening he found himself involved in a minor quarrel over leadership. His hand was forced. He resigned. He joined the Action Group, but the ideas he brought with him marked him as a man to be specially watched. When the North Regional Elections began he went by Land Rover to Gboko and campaigned for the Northern People's Congress. He had by now come to the conclusion that all the political parties were striving towards the same end: freedom from Colonial rule. If only all the parties could put aside their bitterness, frustrations, jealousies, and realize that the end in view was the same . . . but no! everyone wanted to be a leader. Whenever he thought back on those times Wilson always asked himself: If I had not roamed from one political party to the other how could I have developed my present toughness? How could I have seen the last stages in the handing-over of power to Nigeria as the beginning of something much larger in Africa? My IYARI CHEMISTS suffered, but it was worth it. I have been able to see the yoke actually being thrown off, and suddenly Nigeria is free.

Wilson looked ahead and decided: The time has now come to organize something on a much wider scale. The word is 'solidarity', and it has captured my imagination. If there could be solidarity in all Africa . . . but then, again! who will lead? He thought of the old jealousies of the smaller political parties and was sad. The same thing would definitely repeat itself.

4

In her room Yaniya sang quietly to herself. Whenever her mind was troubled she always sang. She had a clear voice and the word 'Jesus' always rang out above the other words in her song. She opened her wardrobe and took down her frocks, spreading them one by one on the bed. She folded her blouses, wrappers, head-ties, and arranged them tightly in one suitcase. Her cocktail dresses she left still hanging in the wardrobe.

In the second suitcase she checked through the food for the children: powdered milk, sugar, chocolate powder, vitamins. She went to the window and looked out. Long cars were pulling up outside. One after another they wrenched and rumbled, then became silent. Men came out of the cars, young men with determined faces and brief-cases tucked under their arms.

Little Lumumba ran into the room, crying: 'Mama, come see! . . . They done come. They done come for Papa house!'

'They're coming for a meeting, Lum!'

Little Pandhit was curled up, asleep. Jomo was tucked close to her. Yaniya put aside the two suitcases and went into the bathroom. Half an hour later Yaniya, wearing a golden bracelet, ear-rings and necklace to match, walked straight through the sitting-room where

Wilson and the leading members of the NMFAMS were smoking and flicking through their papers. Her dress caught their eye by its arresting sheen. They rose and greeted her. Wilson looked at her questioningly, but with a dozen eyes on him he could say nothing. She was out and into the streets.

The car was waiting for her under the trees. Gadson Salifas took her hand and it was trembling.

'Did he see you?' he whispered. 'Did your husband see you, eh, Yaniya?'

'I don't know. . . . Are you afraid?'

She laughed with a whip-lash in her glassy mirth. 'They are at a meeting. The NMFAMS. Think they will reform Africa. Are you afraid?'

'Of your husband or his revolution?' His voice was thick and he held open the door for her. 'I have heard that he employs spies, rabbles, to watch you. Is that true? People who will kill or disable for a mere one pound per day.'

'Be a man,' she said.

She collected the bell-skirt and slipped in, catching her breath. The air within the car filled immediately with the wild aroma of *Balmain*.

'If they come for you, you fight. Don't you think I am worth fighting for? You will only be sacked from the Civil Service. People who take other men's wives have suffered more. Be a man!' She laughed.

'I am afraid for you,' he said. 'I do not want to destroy your family life.'

'There is nothing to destroy. Wilson and I have not spoken for almost three weeks. Is that family life? We live in the same house, you know. . . . And there are children with us. Three of them. You think they don't know what is happening?'

'It is a thing of pity,' he said.

The smile had vanished from his face. She snuggled close, with the lascivious abandon of a female determined to enjoy herself with vindictiveness. The car sped out and away until the tarmac changed to red earth. He took it slowly over the shaky bridge with the water lapping underneath. She saw the single file of men on their bicycles, waiting for them to clear the bridge. Hard-working men returning to their families.

'I feel sinful,' she said. 'But what can I do? I must find happiness.'

He held her hand and squeezed it.

'Mind the road,' she warned, as the car swerved.

He parked the car by the roadside. It was night now and they walked to the Suburban Club. The old man stretched out his hand and Salifas put a coin in it.

'He seems to know you,' she said. 'Do you bring all your women here?'

The old man raised the lantern above his head and led the way.

'This place smells,' she said. 'Why don't we go where you're staying?'

He took her close and kissed her. 'My father suddenly arrived. We cannot meet in my house any longer. This place is all right: just for tonight!'

'You haven't changed,' she said. 'You haven't learned to respect even married women.'

'You are thinking of your snug bedroom and your children. . . . Married women are like that—when they are disloyal to their husbands they think devotedly of their children! . . . Does it give you some consolation?'

There was one bed in the room. He sat on it and Yaniya came and sat on his knee and tugged at his chin. She felt the demanding hands on her breasts.

'I thought you were lecturing me on chastity,' she moaned. 'Have you finished?'

Her fingertips found the prickly hairs on his chin, the furrows on his brow. 'What did you come to do in Lagos?'

'To see you and to take over as senior assistant secretary in the Ministry of Consolation.'

'Tell me, what do you do in the Ministry of Consolation?'

'You don't know? Come, Yaniya. You don't know that our job is to look after Nigerians, men and women in distress, and to console them? Have you not seen pictures of our Minister in the Press at his work of consolation?'

'I remember. It's a big job. I hope you will now settle down and be serious.'

'Go 'way, Yaniya! You know I'm always serious. My wife will soon join me.'

'Which one?' She laughed. 'Gadson Salifas, settling down; isn't it funny?'

He laughed. 'You don't seem to believe me. The one in the U.K. She's completing her course there. I tell you, I'm a serious man now.'

Yaniya laughed. 'When she comes she'll be like the others. Here today, gone tomorrow.'

'You want to be naughty now.' He held her away from him. 'Yaniya, wait. I want to see more of your beauty.' He was toying with the buttons on her blouse. 'You have three children, yet your breast feels like that of a virgin girl.'

'I married early, that's why. I was eighteen when I gave birth to Lumumba. But now I'm an old woman! My husband is not interested in my charms any more. He sees the upright breasts of teenagers in Lagos streets.'

He smiled. 'Do you know that those teenagers vamp men? They actually seek men out and go for them. Not the boys, no! Boys do not interest them. I mean men whom they know have wives and children.'

'I know. . . . Lagos is rotten inside. Before we settled here Wilson was not like that.'

'Like what?'

'Running after upright breasts.'

'Your husband is a famous man,' he said. 'If he does not run after upright breasts upright breasts will run after him. Just imagine: Wilson Iyari, president of the Nigerian Movement for African and Malagasy Solidarity! Women must run after him; and, being famous, he succumbs to their flattery. He's a man, and therefore vain.'

'He's mad,' she said. 'Everybody knows he's mad. He and his beard! Nobody takes him seriously.'

'You love him all the same.'

'That was before, not now.' She turned her back.

He helped her undo the hook that held her skirt.

'Ah!' he exclaimed, momentarily admiring her loveliness. Then he said: 'The way you talk about him makes me sure you still love him. I know.'

'Are you jealous?' she teased. 'He inflames my spirit. I think I now hate him. I'm only with him because . . . to avoid a scandal. And the children, you know. . . . If I were to leave him now, don't you see . . . it will be bad! People will say . . .'

She had taken off her clothes now, and was covering her body inadequately with arms crossed before her. She was a really black girl, tall, and slim and jet black. She had an oblong face, sly, with eyes that did not meet your eyes but slid sideways like billiard balls gently prodded. She had velvet skin, an oblong bottom, balanced by an oblong belly which he fondled lingeringly. He pulled her so she sat on his knees.

'Are you pregnant?' he asked.

She sprang to her feet haughtily. 'Don't ever say it again! My body tires of children!'

He laughed. 'Three children enough? Where's African manpower gone? My mother bore eight.'

'You wish me dead, then? You don't know that the last one nearly killed me dead. What is my life if I am always bearing children? Women like me go to United Nations and speak for Nigeria. How do they exceed me in greatness? Let me rest from children and live my life, *bo*!'

He rubbed her belly, but she shied away from him.

'Please don't touch me! We're talking with seriousness.'

'Come, fiery temper!' He pursued her malewise round the room. He caught her, and she crouched and bounced away from him.

'Please leave me! Woman's body delights you so! Ah! . . . Me pregnant?'

'It's you who delight me, Yaniya, not woman!' His voice trembled. 'You are my mistress and must delight me.'

She laughed, ridiculing his mounting passion. 'So, I delight you? You love me? Say it, let me hear. Do you love all the other women you bring to this filthy place?'

'I tell you there are no others.' He took her hands tenderly. 'Yaniya, you look so beautiful.'

'Because you want to lie with me I am beautiful. Ha! Or is that not what you want?'

'Don't talk like that, Yaniya; it spoils . . . it ruins our

romance. You sound callous, you speak like one whose heart is heavy, who regrets what she is doing. It wounds me to hear your harsh words. We are supposed to be happy.'

'I am sorry,' she said. She came to him and embraced him, fondling his head. 'I don't know what is wrong with me. Inside I am all confused and angry. . . .'

He clung tightly to her, smothering her words.

'Wait,' she said. 'Don't lift me to the bed yet. Let me take off this bracelet. Wilson bought it for me for seventy-five pounds.' His arms slackened. 'You are surprised? It is made by Hooper, the great goldsmith. Oh yes, my husband tries to be kind to me. He buys me things. Everything I need he gives me. But the way he treats my family, I can never forgive him that one.'

'So you want him to marry you, your sisters, brothers, father, mother——'

'Not so. At least he must give them respect.'

'Do you respect his own family? Oh! . . . So that's why you have come here with me? To punish Wilson? I can see that! You have come here because you cannot subject your husband to your every little whim. So you want to make him feel pain by openly flirting. And I am the fool you chose.'

She stroked his chin. 'You really understand women. I wish I could make Wilson know we are here. I want to hurt him bad. I want to do things to pain him. I want to exercise my freedom now, because I have been too quiet. I want to enjoy my life, to live as if no man should control my movements.'

'You are not worried if he finds out?'

'Why should I?' She stood erect, implacable. 'You see, it is not women who are bad, it is men who make women bad. I speak of myself. When Wilson and I were courting I was crazy in love. I never saw other men. There were men before, but when he came I dismissed them all from my mind. All of them. I was loyal. God knows. Then he started. He thought I was a fool. . . . First one girl, then another. I actually found love-letters. We fought. Do you know he beat me, not minding my pregnancy, and I was in hospital three months? All because of a girl friend. And where's she today? Gone off with another man. So why shouldn't I do the same as he does?'

He laughed. 'An eye for an eye, that's equality. Well, I'm lucky you decided to pursue men. But listen. Much as I love you, Yaniya, I will tell you this; for men this kind of love is an adventure. For women it is sure to lead to something else. Something terrible.'

She looked at him sharply. 'Like what?'

'Separation, murder, death of the children . . . something evil, like that. For women it is always so. You watch and see.'

'I don't care,' she said. 'I don't care any more. Come to me and stop your sermon!'

Lights flooded the lane leading to the Country Club and cracked through the windows of the room. Yaniya quickly grabbed her clothes. Hurriedly she dressed and they crowded to the window. They heard a car pull up on the road. A man and a girl came out of it and began walking to the house. The man looked like Wilson Iyari, but the girl was strange. Yaniya went numb. She heard the voice of the man, thick and muffled. She saw the old housekeeper approach the new arrivals and stand with them for a while.

'Do you know them?' Gadson whispered.

'I—I think . . . He looks like my husband.' She was shivering. 'Take me home, quickly!'

He chuckled uneasily. 'You're imagining things! Where's your bravado gone? How can that be your husband? Only few can find their way here. We'll wait till they're gone. They can't come in here.'

5

At the door of her home Yaniya hesitated for a moment, overcome by a flood of guilt. She stood listening to the voices within. They were still at their meeting. Summoning up courage, she pushed the door open. Heavy cigarette smoke hung in the room, with Wilson a mere haze within the fumes. In one brief glance Yaniya saw the map spread on the table, the heads poring over it. She heard clearly the snatch of a decision.

'We shall then march from Tafawa Balewa Square——'

It was the one they called Kwame, the refugee from Ghana, Wilson's deputy. She knew his voice. She shut the door with a bang. They looked up for a moment, their concentration shattered.

'Welcome, Mrs Iyari,' said one.

A sudden feeling of obstinacy against Wilson assailed her. She was full of strength now for her fight against him if he ever dared accuse her of anything. She would fight him to the last.

'Mrs Iyari, welcome. . . .'

She nodded and slipped by.

Behind her the same voice was saying, '. . . Wilson, you will be in charge of those marching from the clock tower towards the House of Reps . . .'

She was in her room. The utter confusion of it bewildered her. On her bedroom locker the clock was registering ten minutes to twelve midnight. Little Lum and Pandhit lay curled in the most exotic attitudes. Jomo lay still, untroubled in his cot. She alone was the outsider in the family of Iyari. She began to take her clothes off one by one for the second time that evening. As she put them away it seemed to her that the furtive and tiring joy she had gone out to buy was being shed away for the reality which now confronted her: pissing children, the wrath of an outraged husband. She touched little Jomo's napkin and found that it was wet. She took it to the sink and changed it. In a moment she had put on the most sophisticated things and got into bed.

Wilson had seen her come in, had noticed the new brightness in her eye. He sat, listening to the talk about African Independence, African Unity, African Culture. . . . The young men in the room talked and argued, but they arrived at no conclusion, save that there must be a demonstration, a peaceful affair.

'Wilson, you will be in charge of those marching from the clock tower, to the House of Reps . . .' He heard the words as his wife passed by. The scent of *Balmain* hung in the air with a snobbery that enraged him. He fixed his eyes on the graceful neck, as if by doing so he could penetrate her innermost thoughts.

He knew she had begun lately to be unfaithful to him. Who could the man be? A newcomer to Lagos? It was such a big city she could begin with one of her former lovers and he would never know. Or was it some small irresponsible lad, a Grade Two clerk in some mercantile office whose entire salary could buy him only one pair of shoes? Women were unpredictable and stupid when it came to furtive affairs. With her three children, she might be fooling with a boy of nineteen for all he knew. Lagos was rapidly becoming Nigeria's divorce centre. It was the mark of its outward sophistication that nowhere did a happy marriage really exist. There was always the other man or the other woman. Marriage had become a sham, a façade, a social show-off. Once in a while husband and wife were seen together in public. Home life had vanished. The husband went on a mission to New York, taking with him a woman to warm his bed, the wife carried her typewriter and flew with policemen to the Congo. That was independence.

Daily he read the divorce cases. Up to this moment, he would never believe they were anything else but mere newspaper sensationalism: NURSING SISTER STEALS DOCTOR HUSBAND. HUSBAND SEES MAN KISSING WIFE IN GARAGE. WOMAN CLAIMS HEAVY DAMAGES IN MARRIAGE BREACH CASE. . . . They could never, in his imagination, involve real identifiable people with flesh and blood. If he was doing something about African Solidarity what was he doing about the disintegration of the Iyari family? His own children, members of his family, Lum, Pandhit, Jomo—they would soon grow up; into what? Disgruntled youths?

Yaniya was doing more harm to his dedicated cause than she ever knew. Deliberately she was working him up into a state of desperation. Suppose he put a stop to it now, strangled her in her bed? But how could it ever be kept quiet? The story would be told how Wilson Iyari, leader of the NMFAMS, murdered his wife. His enemies would capitalize on that. They would go back and trace the development of his mental disintegration.

When the last of the NMFAMS men had left he had the whole house to himself. He locked the doors and went into Yaniya's room. She was not asleep. She was lying lazily curled, her face shining with cream. He was by now used to her frown when she set eyes on him, but what angered him was the way she quickly drew the tail of her night-gown down over her knees, gazing at him with the terrified eyes of a girl about to be raped.

Wilson asked, 'Where did you go?'

'I went for a walk.' She pulled little Pandhit close. 'Where did you go?'

Slowly she sat erect on the edge of the bed. He could see her breasts through the thin night-gown. Yaniya was always correctly dressed, even in bed. A signet-ring sparkled as she lifted her arm.

'Your brother told me in the pharmacy that you are a very loyal wife.'

'Don't bring my brother into this.'

'He said you are a loyal wife and you always speak well of me to people. Did you speak nice things with the man you went to meet?'

'So if I go out it means——'

'If you go out in the early evening, without telling me, and return at midnight . . . look at the clock!'

'If I go out it means to meet a man?' She held her head high with pride. 'Your mind works in only one way. What proof have you? Can't I go and see Brother Jacob? Has it come to that? Am I a prisoner? Please go to your bed and sleep! I'm tired.'

Wilson sprang forward. He raised his arm menacingly. In the early days of their marriage Wilson would have struck her, perhaps wounded her, and they would spend weeks afterwards inventing tales to doctors and friends. But now his hand dropped to his side. He took out a handkerchief and mopped his brow.

'Say what you like. Behave to me as you like. The fact remains: to the world outside I am something. To you I may be nothing. It doesn't worry me. . . . But think also of the children, Jomo, Pandhit and Lum. You are bringing them up to disregard the authority of their father. That's the shameful part of it.' He lowered his voice as little Lum stirred in his sleep. 'Yaniya, if you are tired of living here why don't you just clear out? I mean it. We can arrange about the children. Nobody need know the truth.'

The words were out and in the air, and in the room about him, the potent expression of what he knew she also felt. A terrible challenge. He stood so still that his head began to swim. Nothing was happening to anyone any more. Numb deadness gripped all things living and dead.

'You can have the children. Is that not enough? I don't mind. When they grow up that won't stop them knowing who is their father. They will know also their mother was a useless woman!'

She did not say a word. He waited for her to say something before he plunged deeper into the mess he had now made. She opened her mouth like one struck, and closed it. But there were no words. Two bright streaks wetted her lovely cheeks. He turned and walked slowly to his room. There was a book at his bedside. He opened it and lay back on his bed to read. The print swam before his eyes.

6

IYARI and Kwame, his deputy leader, arrived at the airport before seven in the morning, but it was already crowded. Their car formed part of a long queue and they waited fifteen minutes before a policeman with a stern face waved them into an enclosure.

It began to rain. The sky became muddy and steamy and no one could retire to any shelter because the shelters had been torn down after the Independence Celebration. It was a relief when the aircraft appeared overhead, circled the airport and taxied slowly into position. Everyone waited. The VIP staircase, white in the rain, was wheeled into place. The door of the plane swung open and there stood the Prime Minister, robed, arm raised aloft.

The women broke the cordon. Wives and friends of Ministers charged towards the plane. Wilson turned to Kwame. 'Remember . . . we must stick together.'

The Prime Minister came down the steps and other Ministers appeared. The women surged forward, waving handkerchiefs, clapping with joy. They lined up with the Ministerial group and photographers buzzed about before the Prime Minister led the way to the VIP lounge where the Press waited. He sat down, flanked by two other Ministers. The lights of the film-makers shone into his eyes. He looked tired, but his eyes were alert and his manner calm.

A boy stepped up to the microphone and asked:

'Did you like the President of the U.S.?'

'I like him. I think he is a sincere man.'

'You have been attacked by a Negro paper in the United States for being oblivious to the whole situation of the black man in the world. Is this true?'

'Ridiculous. But don't forget there is a limit to which we can meddle in the internal affairs of a people.'

They were scribbling away. The words spoken by the Prime Minister echoed immediately in the public-address system and everyone present could hear them. Another journalist stepped up to the microphone. He was pushed aside by a man who had not raised his hand. It was a scramble. The Prime Minister had been away for a long time, had been grilled by pressmen as slick as electric eels, men with exaggerated ideas of their own cleverness. He had come through it all with distinction. And now...

'Very recently a Nigerian was refused service in a U.S. restaurant. A distinguished Nigerian. . . . And yet the Americans in Nigeria are given unlimited privileges. . . .'

'You must look at the whole thing calmly, my friend. Incidentally, the President has already apologized about this mistake and the whole matter has been settled. To understand it you have to go back to the history of the American people. We can do little except protest, and that we have done and got redress. Each case has its own peculiarities. Gradually the Government will be forced to legislate; by public opinion. This is a matter for the American Government to decide. Kennedy is doing his best. I met him and we talked of a number of things. How would you feel, for instance, if Americans began interfering in our own domestic problems? No State is perfect, least of all ours. We just have to learn to live with others in spite of their faults.'

Iyari raised his hand. 'May I ask a question, please?'

He stood behind the microphone. Immediately there was a hum. 'NMFAMS! . . .'

'What are we doing about African and Malagasy Solidarity?' The question came out of the blue. The Prime Minister stared at him, then smiled.

'Who is this man?'

'I am Wilson Iyari.'

'And what are those feathers in your cap? What is the meaning of the letters NMFAMS?'

'Nigerian Movement for African and Malagasy Solidarity, sir.'

'Oh! . . . That's why you asked the question!' Everyone laughed. 'You are the man with the beard! . . . I have heard of you. Yes, you are the leader of the Nigerian Movement for African Solidarity. . . .'

Iyari felt uncomfortable, but stood his ground. He wiped his face. A spotlight had been swung round so that it shone full in his face. He was conscious of the TV cameras, the reporters who looked at his lips with pencils poised, shadows of curious bodies filtering about the room.

'Africans must come together,' Wilson said. 'My movement is dedicated to the abolition of disunity. We demand, sir, that you visit each and every State where Africans live, free, or under domination. No country is too large, no country is too small no country is too near, none too far. We demand, sir, that you make a definite effort to bring together all African States and Malagasy.'

While he spoke the Prime Minister's fingers stroked the microphone stand.

'Have you finished? . . . Well, my young leader. If I visited all these people and places—granting that I could find the time—when will I do my work here in Nigeria? You will admit this visiting cannot be done in one day. And then you will start criticizing me. Not that I mind. You are in a hurry and this country is one of freedom of speech. Eh?' The Prime Minister smiled and everyone laughed. 'Anyway, I'll see what can be done.'

Wilson found he was not making the headway he wanted. He sat down. The questions shifted from one journalist to the other. Wilson was no longer interested. He looked at Kwame Amantu and they understood each other. Without further ado, the two men slipped into the background and found their car.

It was during the drive back that morning from the airport that Wilson and Kwame decided that too long had they been taken lightly by the authorities. They must now go ahead and stage a public demonstration. They must find out for themselves the general feeling of the people.

Wilson and his men were gathered in his sitting-room. Wilson was talking, while the hawkers sold the evening kerosene outside and the buses were taking the cinema-goers to see the latest Indian films.

'I hope you all know what we're demonstrating for. We are decided to demonstrate, aren't we?'

'African Solidarity,' came the chorus.

'Yes, and more than that,' said Wilson. 'We are demonstrating to bring it to the notice of the leaders of all African countries that none of them can afford to sit back and ignore the call for unity. Africa united could constitute a force to be reckoned with. Disunited, it breaks into a handful of suffering millions, with nothing effective about them.'

Beside him sat his deputy, Kwame, pulling away at his cigarette. The others in their robes were still as statues, listening.

Wilson warmed to his theme. 'Colonialism is gone, but separatist influences are at work. Let Nigeria set an example by smashing them before all Africa. We are already united internally——'

'Unite Africa!' came the chorus.

Wilson was surprised. He remembered the CID men who had been patrolling the outside of his house and wondered when they would break into the room and seize the documents.

'Solidarity is imperative. We don't care how difficult it is. It is a possibility. Africa can reach unity much more easily than any other continent; and this is the time, now!'

As he mentioned the word 'solidarity' Wilson saw the door of the bedroom open. His wife, resplendent, came out, passed through the sitting-room, and before they could rise to greet her she was outside, leaving a bewitching trail of *Balmain*.

The men exchanged glances. One of them said, 'I hope we have not upset Mrs Iyari. . . .'

Wilson shook his head. 'No . . . it—it gets lonesome and uncomfortable in there. . . .'

'Why don't we ask her? Sometimes I feel women can contribute a lot.'

Wilson glanced at his deputy. 'A good idea. Oh, we will form a women's wing, but not at this stage.'

She is going to meet her lover, Wilson thought. *I talk*

about solidarity. There it is! My own family split. But how can Africa be united when such a small unit as my family is not united?

A loud cry came from the bedroom. Wilson excused himself and went in to see Little Lum bathed in tears. He placed a hand on the boy's temple and it was fiery hot. This boy was ill. Wilson was terrified. There were no drugs in the house, and the attack could be anything from pneumonia to malaria. The wisest thing was to take him at once to a doctor.

The door was half open and he could hear the drifting words: '... We are going to confront the authorities with our plans for African Solidarity...'

'No, that is not our business. Our business is to present the Government with the voice of youth. We are the mouthpiece of modern Africa...'

The boy seemed to have calmed down and Wilson laid him down and covered him carefully. He went back to the meeting.

'... But your meetings have been banned. You cannot meet in public. Under the emergency regulations the Prime Minister has called off all public meetings.'

'We just have to defy the order.'

'And take the consequences?'

'Sure!'

Brother Jacob laughed and Wilson looked sharply at him. He remembered the fourteen borrowed pounds and knew he would never see them again. He thought of Brother Jacob's sister, his wife. Where had she gone? And immediately he felt an anger all about him.

'We are free!' said someone. Something about this meeting was beginning to irritate Wilson.

'You are free!' came a challenging voice from the back. 'Yes! You are free. Where is your right of free speech, your right of assembly? How free are you?'

'It's only an Emergency Order. It will soon be lifted.'

'They are afraid of us. Look! You know what I saw? As I was coming I saw a plain-clothes man outside the door. He's still there now. What is he watching? Isn't he interested in African Unity?'

There was laughter. A glass of beer was lifted to thirsty lips. A bottle was carelessly opened and the contents frothed and spilled.

Wilson held his throbbing head. 'Listen. All those who believe in African Solidarity will come forward. Oh yes. They'll give money. They'll give moral support. They'll do everything in their power. This is going to be a peaceful demonstration, that's all. If they don't understand what a peaceful demonstration is——'

'Everyone interested will take part in the rally!' said Brother Jacob. 'You don't need to be a member of the NMFAMS to take part in the demonstration! Forget the ban! If the police get tough it's just too bad!'

More wild laughter and confusion. A man said, 'Tear gas, batons . . . what shall we do?' and the question was drowned in cigarette smoke. 'Nothing! . . . We do not believe in violence. . . .'

'We shall continue our work if imprisoned.'

'What shall we call it? Demonstration for Solidarity of African and Malagasy States? . . .'

'No,' said Brother Jacob. 'Too long.'

Kwame held a glass of beer aloft. 'I've got it! Let's call it Africa Day Demonstration! Africa Day Demonstration. . . .'

Someone behind said, 'Trust a Ghanaian to think up

big names!' and Kwame looked at him with fire in his eyes.

'The date of the demonstration,' said Wilson. 'Let's say October One, Nigeria's Independence Day. Are we agreed?'

'Why October One?' asked Brother Jacob.

'To tell Africa that the largest African nation is sponsoring the move; and not only that——'

The words were taken out of his mouth and the hubbub became deafening. So hot had the room become that everyone started pulling their robes off, leaving them in only jumpers and baggy trousers.

Wilson called Kwame to his side and whispered to him, 'This is the time to show them the placards. . . .'

Kwame had a pile of them and he banged the table and they listened while he displayed them.

UNITED AFRICA CAN ALTER THE BALANCE OF THE WORLD.

IDEAS NEED NO PASSPORTS: OUR IDEA IS AFRICAN SOLIDARITY.

Kwame paused, but no one commented on either of the placards.

PERSONALITY CULT BRINGS PERSONALITY CLASH: WORK FOR UNITY NOT SELF.

'Hio, hio!' came a chorus.

They talked about the placards, arguing far into the night. Everyone felt they were too long and wordy. For the Africa Day Demonstration they must be short, to the point and bold. The most popular one was:

PERSONALITY CULT BRINGS PERSONALITY CLASH: WORK FOR UNITY NOT SELF.

When they had all agreed on the wording Wilson was relieved. Kwame drank a glass of beer and boasted it was his own original phrasing. While they were still trying to decide what to do with it, Wilson heard distinctly the cry of his little son. There was nothing for it this time. He must take him to the hospital. If only his mother was back. It was getting on for the early hours and now a light drizzle had begun.

Cool gusts of wind blew the lonely leaves across the road. Like a lover, the drizzle had crept upon the night, quietly fertilizing the earth. The steaming vapour rose from the earth, baked and thirsty with weeks of dryness, eager to be fecundated. The languorous arms of Yaniya, female, supple as the twining plant, clung round her lover's neck. His wet lips mumbled obscenities.

She breathed a sigh. 'When it rains like this I want a man. I want the smell of man's sweat in my nose.'

He crushed her to him till she groaned.

'You are happy now? We're much safer here. Nobody will disturb us.'

'I'm not happy,' she said.

'Why not?' He pulled away from her.

'Happiness is of the mind, not body. . . . Since I met you I have been able to find no peace. I keep thinking of you the whole day. I keep hating my husband all the more. It was never like this. I never hated him before. He is kind to me as always, and considerate; but his very kindness irritates me, and I keep hating him. But it is not making me happy.'

He did not say anything.

'You see, when you do evil—as we are doing now—it is sweet only when you know somebody is watching you; or that if you are caught you will suffer; and if you do not care any more. If your heart has become like stone.

I know my heart is not like that. My husband does not watch me. He does not have time to care what I do. But I want to do something to make him care, to wound his vanity. And I cannot. He is above me in that, and it pains me. But I want it to hurt him. What shall I do?'

She began to weep. He held her. She let his hands pass over her wet face. She let him hold her for a long time. Then she got up from the bed and began putting on her clothes, extravagant, fashionable, frilly. She looked tall and graceful and smelt sweet.

He crept up behind her.

'It never tires me to look at your beautiful body.'

'Your wife will soon be back, and then you will forget me. It's natural. And it's better that way. Don't tell me anything about her. I don't want to think of that time, yet. I only want to remember this wonderful time with you. It is painful too.'

Through their conversation the piercing cry of a child intruded like a punishment. Yaniya heard it clearly and almost ran to the door, forgetting she was not in her own home.

She stood still, clutching her heart. 'I—I thought it was Lumumba. God! . . .'

'Lumumba?'

'That's our son. . . . Wilson said he would call all our children after famous Nationalists in Africa or Asia. We have a girl called Pandhit, and the youngest boy, Jomo, after Kenyatta.' Unknown to her a softness and warmth had crept into her voice.

'I can see you love your children.'

'Very much. Wherever I go I take their memory with me. . . .'

'You are going somewhere?'

'I don't know yet, I am so unhappy. When I feel like this I think of my father in the forest who loves me. Ol' Man Forest, they call him. But his real name is Emorwen. I want to be a little girl. I want to be loved and important.'

They did not talk much during the drive home. Gadson Salifas made one attempt, but Yaniya only half heard him. As soon as he put her down she again became intolerably lonely.

Instead of going home she began walking till she came to Tafawa Balewa Square where the Independence Anniversary decorations shone in the false light. Already the celebrations were near. She stood under one of the banners while a car drove past. It was after it had gone that Yaniya recognized it as Wilson's. The meeting of the NMFAMS must have ended. She concluded that he must be taking some members to their homes.

She hailed the first taxi she saw and hurried home.

As Wilson entered the hospital carrying his sick son in his arms, heads turned and the name Iyari was whispered by all. He nodded and walked towards a bench and the people seated on it shifted so he could find a space. The nurse who was sterilizing instruments did not so much as look at him. An orderly came to him and told him to go to another part of the hospital where he would obtain a card. Wilson put his hand on the boy's cheek. His temperature was rising.

He joined the queue waiting to be given cards. After a long while he obtained a card, then came back and sat on the bench. A pretty nurse came, examined the boy, asked questions. She looked efficient as she took down the answers Wilson gave.

While they sat, Wilson noticed a Nigerian girl who was sitting beside an Englishman on a bench opposite. The girl's eyes were fixed on him throughout, until young Lum had been injected with the drug. Wilson racked his memory, and at last it came. This was the same girl who had spoken with him that evening outside the pharmacy. He could not now speak with her because his son demanded all his attention.

'Don't worry,' said the gentle voice of the doctor. 'Your son will be all right, Mr Iyari.'

When Wilson looked again he found that the girl and the white man had gone.

He and Kwame carried little Lum out. In the streets the air was sweet and clean. Wilson breathed more peacefully. They were walking towards the car when Kwame touched Wilson on the sleeve of his robe.

'Your wife is here.'

Wilson did not speak. He stood by the car, smouldering with anger, the sick boy in his arms. He saw Yaniya, glamorous in this atmosphere of pain and sorrow. She held her head low. Her eyes were full of shame and anxiety.

Kwame opened the door of the car and she went in and sat in front. Wilson sat with the child at the back and Kwame took the wheel. Yaniya was asking questions all along and Kwame answered in monosyllables. Wilson was disinterested.

He thought: I have no wife, really. There's neither peace nor unity in my family. Beautiful Feathers. I am no better than Latifu, my mechanic. He earns eight pounds a month and he can keep a wife.

The car stopped. Kwame ran to his side and opened the door. Yaniya took the child from him and went indoors. He was not quite sure, but he thought he saw a wetness on her face.

He was strangely touched. He let her enter her room and he stood outside talking with Kwame.

'If it were possible for me to stay home and mind the children I would do so. But it is not a man's work. I have no more faith in Yaniya. No more. Her life is outside. Imagine!'

Kwame looked at the ground, not raising his head. 'Women are complex,' he said. 'You know what? If I were you I would find a good nanny.'

'They're hard to get, the good ones,' Wilson said. 'But I must try, for the sake of the children.'

'Yes, I hear the Labour Exchange can help.'

'The Labour Exchange?'

'Oh yes. . . . Girls, elderly women . . . you can get them through the Exchange. Let's go there in the morning.'

In the morning they tried and got a girl of eighteen, who spent most of her time in the bathroom washing her already fine skin till it shone. Then she spent the rest of the day before Yaniya's mirror, using her mistress's make-up, curling her hair with the curlers, varnishing her nails and painting her lips. When she wheeled the children in the pram no one ever knew where she went, or whether she ever found time to feed the children and to change their clothes. She was too young and beautiful and too well versed in the ways of dancing the twist and highlife to worry about mundane things like baby nursing. When Wilson spoke to her she gave him the corners of her eyes and wiggled away from him challengingly, with a know-all air.

They employed an elderly woman and she was solid

and reliable for the first few days. After that she spent all the time in the hospital with backache, kidney trouble and weak eyes as her primary complaints. When she began to enumerate the secondary complaints Wilson leaned against the wall for support. The shock was unbearable. The children remained neglected.

Once the nanny—in her bright moment—taught Wilson how to prepare *ewedu* soup with fish and vegetables. It was like living with a paid grandma. Wilson's hope revived but soon faded when the very next day she packed her bundle and said she was going back to her son whose wife needed her services.

Wilson found it all very unsatisfactory. He could not concentrate on the NMFAMS. Lum became ill again and had to be admitted into hospital. Often Kwame and Wilson went to see him. Soon, the doctor said, he would be well. Soon.

Wilson was glad to hear the doctor speak so hopefully, because the day of the demonstration was at hand.

7

WILSON arrived at the pharmacy in the morning. This was the quiet hour, when everyone had gone to work in the commercial and industrial areas of Lagos. His pharmacy, situated as it was in the residential area, did little business by day. On the street the housewives were going to market and at the bus stops the queues were getting thinner after the first morning rush. Wilson generally spent this hour making telephone calls and going into town to replenish his stores, do his banking, chat about the profession with old friends.

He parked his car with the air of a man who is glad his son has just come out of hospital. At the gate he saw Kwame, who looked at him anxiously.

'We have been waiting for you.'

He took Wilson by the hand, urgently. The room was full and the NMFAMS members were going through their papers uneasily. Wilson heard the sound of the cash register in the retail shop. This, he thought, was the shop on which he and Yaniya had hoped to build their future happiness.

He sat down and listened.

'The important thing about this demonstration,' Kwame said, 'is peacefulness. You understand? I'm sure our leader Wilson Iyari does not mean it to be anti-American, or pro-Chinese, or anything. . . . We just want to attract the attention of the world at this time. That's all. Fight no one. Turn the other cheek, if necessary. . . .'

As Kwame spoke, Wilson noticed the intensity with which the others listened. Here indeed was a good deputy should anything happen to him. One of the boys raised his hand and asked a question, which Kwame disposed of with a smoothness that was reassuring. But beneath it all Wilson could feel that these boys were at last craving to march.

'Tomorrow afternoon, at three . . .'
'African Solidarity . . .'
'African Solidarity . . .'

They rose, and Wilson drove into town to do his shopping and his banking and gossiping. He even visited the Bank of America, which they were to smash later next evening, and spoke to the manager. On the way he saw Ken Johnson, a first secretary at the American Embassy. Ken waved at him and moved towards his black Chev. When he drove away Wilson knew he was heading for the offices of the United States Information Service.

Wilson drove around uncertainly. Finally he called on the manager of the Good Health Pharmacy, who talked about the new encroachment. Patent-medicine vendors, he said, were selling sulpha drugs, antibiotics, habit-forming drugs. Doctors were prescribing and dispensing their own medicines. It was unthinkable. Where did the pharmacist stand? How could pharmacists ever survive? The manager sat in his ancient store, which smelt of essential oils, and complained, with his glasses threatening to fall off the tip of his nose. As he talked he had a habit of gripping Wilson on the shoulder and wrenching at his clean white robes. The doctors drew a line. The patent-medicine dealers drew a line. The nurses drew a line. The pharmacists stood on the border, essential to all, feared by all, victimized by all. It was unthinkable.

'What shall we do?'

Wilson stared back at him.

There must be something, the manager went on. There must be *something*. Look round Lagos. Instead of diminishing, the pharmacies were actually increasing in numbers. New manufacturing establishments were being set up.

By this time Wilson was no longer listening. He was thinking of the route of the demonstration, feeling the public reaction. He was uncertain of the outcome of tomorrow afternoon at three.

He drove his car near the Central Police Station, and for the first time since they started the preparations he saw a shocking sight. The riot police were massing. He could not believe that he was looking at steel helmets, batons and shields. It could not be true.

Of one thing he was certain: no one would ever declare assemblies on this Independence Anniversary 'unlawful'. To celebrate the anniversary, people must mass. To demonstrate, Wilson must also mass his men.

Towards noon Wilson drove homewards. He had been harbouring an uneasy feeling and now as he came out of his car he was struck with a feeling of emptiness. He pushed open the front door. The door creaked and swung on its hinges, like the fragments of a burglary. He walked from one room to the next. He entered Yaniya's bedroom. An emptiness gripped him hollow. Gone. Yaniya gone. Little Lum? Gone. . . . Little Pandhit? Gone too, with mother. Jomo? He had no choice. They had all forsaken him. Gone. The nanny stared at him.

The Missus had ordered a taxi, she said. The taxi came, just as Masta left for the pharmacy. *I thought you knew.*

So she was running away? I did not guess.

Missus took the children into the taxi and it drove them away. The children were weeping. She carried a box too.

Wilson felt numb. He was sure that she had gone to the home of Brother Jacob. She could not have gone far, he kept repeating. In a blind rage he drove to the suburbs. Brother David met him at the door. He had not seen Yaniya. Brother Jacob had gone to mass his demonstrators and was not to be seen anywhere. Where could Yaniya have gone? Wilson saw now that her very presence had been something. He saw how stubborn, heartless, stupid and proud he had been, thus to ignore his wife, to disregard her very existence.

There was a fat-bottomed girl in the house of Brother Jacob and Wilson heard Brother David call her Agnes. She wore a transparent shirt and jeans and she wriggled her fat bottom. Her hair was matted and uncombed and her face oily. She looked Wilson over with a hard contemptuous stare. She lit a cigarette and said, 'You want my man, he's not here.'

Wilson smiled. Agnes was the type of girl whom Brother Jacob kept. Tomorrow it would be Cecilia or Angelina or Vicki. From this unsteady and fluid background he picked up the words of advice he was so fond of giving whenever Wilson quarrelled with his sister.

By night Wilson had given up the search for Yaniya and concluded that she was either well hidden in the city or well on her way out of it. The night breeze stirred the window blinds and rustled the leaves of the trees. Wilson turned the pages of the book he was trying to read. '*Religious people act with rigorous care . . . conscientiously . . . in ritual or in the attainment of certain inner states . . . This rigorous care in devotion, services, and observances aims at a bond between man and an ultimate Being or Power. . . .*'

He put the book aside. If only he could acquire that 'inner state' nothing would ever touch him. Nothing. That was the great trouble with Africa today, he thought. In the old days the African had a bond with an Ultimate Being. Then came 'civilization', that took away the older religion and substituted something new and unstable. Now that which the white man had substituted was gone. There was nothing. At moments like this the New Black Man—he was one of them—was alone. Alone.

He heard a knock at the door and Kwame came in.

'Wilson, how's things?'

'I can't sleep, Kwame.'

'Neither can I.' Kwame looked around the house and said: 'It appears empty. Did you send her away—for safety? And the children?'

Wilson shook his head. He was close to tears. 'Kwame, I am very worried. My wife has run away.'

'Did you quarrel?'

'No. But we've not been so happy lately. We were like strangers.'

'She'll come back,' said Kwame, and the way he said it made Wilson look up. He felt a ray of hope.

'I am worried about Lum. He has not been well. Just come out of hospital. If she was to run why did she not leave the children behind?'

Kwame shook his head. 'You don't understand, eh? She loves them.' He held Wilson on the shoulder.

'I love the boy too much. And he is still weak——'

'She'll come back. She knows you love the boy, that's why she took him. Have patience. She'll come back. She just wants to punish you.'

Wilson said: 'I have been to Brother Jacob, but he's not back; and she's not there. Where could she have run to?'

Kwame shrugged. 'To her mother, or father. Or to friends! Does a man know where an angry woman runs to? Does she herself even know? She just runs!'

'And takes the children, not minding the danger? With all this death on our roads? To her father, did you say? To her father?'

Yaniya's father lived in Benin, away from the trunk roads, in a village of his own which they called Emorwen's Kingdom. If Yaniya had taken the children there—to that forest—he would never forgive her.

'Wilson,' Kwame said. 'I knew you in our days together at Achimota College. Remember? You were the young Nigerian student with the beard and the stubborn frown. We were in the Accra Home Guard together, and you used to play hockey against my team. . . .'

Wilson rose and began bustling around the house.

'What is it, aren't you going to listen?'

'I want to get you something to drink.'

Kwame said: 'Thank you. You don't mind if I sleep here, do you?' He gathered the folds of his cloth and sank into the divan.

'When I saw you in that *kente* I knew you must be homesick for Ghana.'

Wilson brought the beer on a tray. Kwame poured

it out slowly, and when he had taken a sip he wiped his lips. 'Wilson, you remember how we met, and how I admired your honesty and forthrightness? . . . Well, that's a long time ago, but I still admire such genuine qualities.'

Wilson drew his chair close. He lit a cigarette, wondering what Kwame was trying to say. Was he planning to back out of the demonstration? At this late hour?

'I started thinking, Wilson; and I said to myself: Suppose I am killed tomorrow? What an end! in Nigeria!'

Wilson seized him by the hand. 'You mustn't think like that!'

Kwame brushed his hand aside. 'Why not? I tell you this. We are just like thieves. A thief plans to rob somebody. The plan is wonderful. When he gets to the house the unexpected destroys his plans and he is caught and jailed. We must think of the unexpected. Do you think thieves like to be caught?'

'No,' said Wilson. 'But——' he began, and sprang to his feet. 'If anything should happen to us—you and me . . .'

Kwame took another sip. 'Demonstrators don't like to be shot. But usually they are shot. How's ours going to be different?'

A cold chill gripped Wilson. He passed his dry tongue over his upper lip. 'I—I never thought of it . . . it never occurred to me in that manner at all. At all. I never allowed myself to think of it. . . . You see I've just been re-reading something, to give me inner strength. . . .'

'However, you know how I came to Nigeria. . . . I was a teacher at this school in Mfantsipin. I joined an opposition party. The ruling party did not like the idea. I was detained, imprisoned, shot at. Look at this scar. I've never shown it to you, but this is a fateful night and you might as well see it.'

Kwame lifted his *kente* and Wilson saw the mark above the thigh.

'Three months in hospital. Oh, life was uncomfortable. But through the help of friends I fled and came here. When I got here I saw how you were: a kind of rebel too. I knew you would always be like that. Honest and forthright, but free. That's what I liked. Your freedom. No one imprisoned you for your views, no one shot at you, no one deported you. That's why I threw in my lot with you. Well, tomorrow is our test.'

'Tomorrow is our test,' Wilson repeated. He was seeing a new Kwame this night and for some reason it all seemed prophetic. Suppose Kwame died tomorrow? Trampled by hordes of people, knocked on the head by a police baton ... for there must be police. He stopped pacing. He was going to call the whole thing off. Was it still possible to do so?

'If I survive I must go back to Ghana. I love Nigeria. But Ghana is my home. No matter how bad things have been for me Cape Coast is my homeland. I cannot solve the problem by running away. Better to die like a man—but in my own country. . . . So that's one thing I would like you to know. I shall give you my full support for tomorrow, but after that I must plan to re-enter Ghana. I know they are simply waiting for me, but I must return.'

Wilson could say nothing to this. He had often thought of Kwame, who was a true disciple of African Solidarity, a great sportsman. Once in Ghana, when Lagos defeated Accra at football, Kwame condemned all his countrymen who rose up in arms against the Nigerian team. Such men were very rare and Wilson was particularly proud of him.

They did not pursue the subject any further. Wilson was full of thoughts of his little son Lum and of Little Pandhit, and Jomo. He could still not make out why Yaniya had decided to run away from home in the manner she had done and at this particular time.

8

They massed at the National Stadium and carried the coffin from the stadium to the War Memorial Park. It was here that Wilson Iyari stood on a rostrum and talked to the people. 'The demonstration must be peaceful. All we want is to draw attention to African Solidarity. We want leaders all over Africa to unite. African Solidarity!'

'African Solidarity!' came the chorus.

Wilson waved his arm, and with banners flying they marched. They sang. Melted away was the fear which had gripped him the night before. If a bullet were to whistle through the air and lodge in his ribs he would die happy and go to heaven. He believed that.

While the police band was playing on the race-course the NMFAMS were marching, bearing down towards the centre of the city. Coffin lifted high, placards screaming, they marched towards the palace, following the edge of the lagoon. Wilson waved them onwards.

It was when they began approaching Tafawa Balewa Square where the Anniversary Celebrations were going on that police officers obstructed their path. Wilson and his men, in a fever, pressed on. The police stood firm and called, 'Disperse!'

The procession gathered anger. At this moment word went round. 'They're going to attack us!'

'Calm now. . . . Peaceful demonstration, remember!' shouted Wilson.

A lorry raced up the street and began discharging its passengers—men in uniform and steel helmets. They hastily formed themselves into a fighting group.

Wilson and Kwame were standing side by side when the explosion occurred. 'Disperse!' The sharp order flashed again.

Wilson staggered to his feet and when he was again able to see, Brother Jacob was standing beside him. They broke into a run and gained a side street. From the street corner a car swerved and made towards them, driving straight up the road. Wilson grabbed a stone and hurled it at the car windows and the windows smashed. A man came out of the car, bleeding. Wilson recognized him. It was Ken Johnson, First Secretary at the American Embassy. All about him Wilson was hearing the resounding thunder of stone on glass. Someone was singing a war-song.

Brother Jacob said: 'Let us wound this American. He is an enemy of African Solidarity.'

Wilson held Brother Jacob. 'No.'

From the car a woman slid out and clung to Ken Johnson, her eyes wide with terror. It was Martha Johnson.

'Say, what you planning to do?' asked Ken Johnson.

Wilson said: 'You are an American, and you believe in dollars. You think that with your dollars you can buy up all the goodwill in Africa.'

'Is he a communist?' Martha Johnson stammered. 'He must be a communist, Ken.'

Ken Johnson turned to his wife and said: 'Maybe. I think he's one of these young radicals——'

'Are all of them like that?'

'No, darling. . . . He's one of these chaps who fancy themselves as revolutionaries, kind of——'

Wilson laughed. 'A communist! Grow up!'

'Listen, Willie. Don't talk in this manner. I know how you feel. You're my friend——'

'As a person, yes. As a diplomat, no!'

Martha Johnson drew closer to her husband. 'He looks dangerous, Ken. What shall we do?'

At this moment a mob of demonstrators entered the street from the other end. Ken Johnson and his wife stood perplexed for a moment, then raced for cover, closely pursued by a dozen youths. Wilson shouted at them to come back, but they did not listen to him. A police officer caught up with the leader and pelted him with his baton. The baton splintered and the leader fell to the ground and lay still.

Brother Jacob said: 'You see that? Wilson. You see that? You stand there talking grammar and they're killing your men. And you talk of peaceful demonstration. Let's go! Let's go, one time!'

They picked their way through the streets littered with branches, palm fronds, stones and sticks. Once Iyari stopped to pick up a picture of Abdul Nasser—one of those used to decorate the streets at this anniversary when all African leaders were remembered. Nasser's hair had lost its slickness and the smile was faded, but the determined magnetic eyes were still there.

By now Wilson's men had all broken up into groups. One group marched along Azikiwe Street. On the street they met a beautifully dressed young woman trailing three children.

'That's Zuma,' Brother Jacob said.

Zuma was the widow of a Nationalist who died in an anti-colonialist demonstration a year before Independence. They stopped her.

She smiled uneasily. 'What is happening in the town? Can a woman not come out or go peacefully about?'

'Zuma,' said Brother Jacob, 'we want you to do something for us. Take these stones. Throw them at that building.'

She smiled, wheeled on her stiletto heels and shading her eyes with her hands looked the building over. 'If my husband were alive would he approve?'

'Yes, yes! He would! He was a great enemy of "divide and rule".'

She hesitated. 'I am a widow. I look among you and see no friend of my late husband's. He sacrificed his life for politics. What have you people done for me since he died? What have you done for his children?'

'This is not the time, Zuma. This is not the time. We're in a hurry. Are you or are you not for us? You must throw the stones. It must be you who threw the stones. That will be something to tell. Zuma, the politician's widow, threw stones at a foreign bank building and shattered the glass windows. . . .'

Her eyes brightened. 'I am for you. I am for African Solidarity. My husband was an enemy of Colonialism. Colonialism has been defeated. Now it is time to unite. But are you for me?' . . . She looked over the mob with hard eyes. 'Are you for me? You have all been too busy fighting for your own pockets. . . . You want me to break the windows of the foreign bank and the capitalist bank. . . . Well, give me the stones! I shall do as you wish. God knows, I am not throwing the stones for you, but for the cause of African Solidarity . . .' She took the stones in her beautiful fingers, wiping off the sand and polishing the jagged edges. 'My life has been one long battle since my husband died. I maintain the children. I maintain the good name of my late husband. God forbid that I do anything against his name.'

One of the little boys held her by the skirt. She was shapely without being fat, and she looked well. Her hair was thick and glossy. She moved with a rhythm long since forgotten by the younger generation. She bore her head proudly.

'Give me the stones. You people fight for your own cause! Each man wants to lead, that is the trouble. You're not ashamed.'

They gave her more stones and moved back to give her room. She swung her arm back and like lightning the stone sped away and crashed against the window of the bank building. The group cheered. Brother Jacob ran forward and with a large bar crashed open the door and they all scampered up the steps and began to help themselves.

Once Brother Jacob looked outside and saw the Land Rovers of the Federal Police with their aerials and loudspeakers. Every one of them was packed full with demonstrators on their way to the police station. As they drove off, the mob smashed the glass window of a bicycle shop and rushed in. A moment later men were mounting new bicycles and riding away into the town.

One group caught the white man who was driving towards the square. He had a black girl by his side. She was cute. From the white man's calm bearing they could see that he must be a man of some standing.

He stopped the car, and the men seized the Nigerian girl, who was dressed in very tight clothes, with her arms and the tops of her breasts exposed. She was dressed in this provocative manner and was sitting beside a white man. One of the group, a man with hairs on his chest, tore her blouse straight down the front so that everyone saw her young breasts pointing downwards like new mangoes. She covered her breasts, but the man tore her arms aside and they began to struggle and he tripped her. They rolled on the ground with others looking on and now the man was tearing away her skirt amid yells of encouragement.

Wilson arrived in a car bearing the letters NMFAMS. He jumped down. 'Leave her, you beast!' He slapped the hairy-chested maniac, whose eyes now shone with lust. 'Peaceful demonstration, not rape! Not looting!'

The girl was in a state of shock. Wilson put her and the white man in the car and ordered the driver to take them to the Minister.

'Thank you, I thought I recognized you. You're Wilson Iyari, Leader of the NMFAMS. I'm the Perennial Secretary to the Ministry of Consolation. . . .'

He had lost his pipe in the scuffle, and was now coatless. They left his car, with the shattered windows and the ripped-open tyres, under a mango tree.

The girl whom Wilson had rescued was Chini, secretary-typist to the Ministry. She was slick and beautiful and modern, with an Independent Africa finish. Her eyes were red from her recent encounter and she clutched her blouse protectively. Wilson was sure he had seen her before. And then he remembered: Chini, the girl who attended the evening classes near the pharmacy, the girl who had once come out of the traffic and the evening rush to say how much she admired him. He stroked his beard contentedly.

'Where to?' asked the driver.

'To the Minister's house.'

The driver avoided the large streets and in a few moments their car emerged at the junction of two streets, one of which led to the Minister's house. Wilson noticed the traffic policeman on point duty at the intersection, and thought, rather unusual! When the car stopped the officer peered into it and opened the door on Wilson's side.

'Excuse me, sah,' he said, quite polite in manner. 'You are Mr Wilson Iyari.' He referred to a photograph which he drew from his breast pocket.

Wilson sat forward. 'Yes, officer.'

'We want you at the police station,' the officer said. 'We have instructions to bring you when we see you. . . . Sorry, sah!'

Wilson was touched. Here was an officer who was obviously a sympathizer but who must do his duty.

'You mean you arrest me?'

'Just so, sah. Sorry, sah!' He helped Wilson down, shut the door and the car drove on. Wilson saw the friendly hand of Chini waving at him through the window. He had become a hero. He stood there watching the NMFAMS car carrying Chini towards the Minister's house. A patrol car was coming towards them. The man at the wheel did not smile.

'You give us plenty trouble,' he said.

Wilson looked at him coldly. 'Come on, inside!'

Wilson clambered into the vehicle while the friendly policeman said: 'Gently, sah. Sorry, sah!'

9

THE Minister of Consolation was standing before the mirror admiring his own image. He turned his face to the left and smiled. He turned his face to the right and smiled. He watched the mirror to see the effect of smiling with his teeth shut tight, with his lips parted and his tongue lolling out.

In the mirror he saw the image of his Complimentary Secretary. 'What is it now?'

'Your Perennial Secretary to see you, sir!'

'Tell him I'm busy.' He studied his profile and adjusted his cap. There was a flash of light. A photographer had taken a picture. The Minister struck a pose. There was another flash of light. The photographer cranked his camera.

'You must see him, sir,' said the Complimentary Secretary. 'He is very worried. I think they beat him, sir.'

'Beat him? Where?'

'In the riot, sir.'

'Awright, but I can only see him for a minute.'

The Perennial Secretary came in with his hands behind his back, his clothes in tatters. 'So sorry, sir.'

'What happened?'

'Nothing, really. . . . I was driving towards your honourable residence when I was waylaid by a group of rioters. They stopped the car, pulled me out and beat me. They fell on the girl, with intent to assault her. But for Wilson Iyari——'

'Where did this happen?'

'Near the race-course.'

'I'm sorry to hear that. You want to go home now, or——'

'No, it's nothing at all, sir.'

'All right, then. I want you to write me a speech, quickly.' He glanced at the mirror. 'Don' make it too long. Any speech!'

The Perennial Secretary was prepared. He sat in a corner of the lounge and drafted a speech which he took along to the Minister, who was still standing before the mirror.

'Thank you.' He smiled, and with flourishes read the speech to the mirror, making appropriate gestures.

Hearing a noise, the Minister asked, 'Who are those?'

Indeed, his courtyard was filling up with a crowd of men, women with children on their backs, glamour girls in slacks. They came into the lounge and sat on the best chairs. Some of them drifted into the dining-room and began helping themselves to the meal laid out on the table. Some of them had addressed envelopes in their hands.

'The usual crowd, sir,' said the Perennial Secretary. 'From your constituency. Would you like to see them, sir?'

'Be tactful. . . . Tell them no jobs for them *as yet*.'

One of those carrying an addressed envelope burst into the room. 'But, Minister, one of our brodder who come here last week—you gave him job.' His clothes were an embarrassment. He held his stomach and rolled his eyes. 'We are hungry. We hear that plenty work come out in the Ministry of Consolation. So we hear.'

The Minister smiled and shook his head. He dipped his hand into his wallet and held up six pound notes. 'Tha's the last I have. Take and divide among yourselves. I will not hide work from you if there is work. Is what I'm here for. To see that you don' suffer. After all, I represent you.'

'Thank you, sir. Next election you will go in—by the power of our vote.'

'By the power of God,' corrected another man, breaking into the room, and now there were twenty of them waving envelopes addressed to the Minister. 'It is God who above everything.'

'Just so. Next time you will go in by the power of God—and our vote.'

The Perennial Secretary appeared and stood with his hands behind his back. When they had drifted back into the compound he observed, 'They're always the same, these people from your constituency.'

'They're nice people. If you explain to them some will understand, some will not. Some think I have the power to manufacture jobs. I am just a servant, like you.'

The Perennial Secretary laughed. 'Hardly the same, sir.'

'They vote me into power,' said the Minister, 'so I mus' respect them.' He became serious suddenly. 'Write me another speech at once. The first one is not strong. I want a strong one this time.'

'What about, may I ask, Mr Minister?'

'Just write me a speech.'

'Yes, sir.'

The Perennial Secretary held his aching head and in between groans set about writing another speech. He had been an administrative officer in his time. Independence had not dampened his love for Nigeria, which now prevented him from electing to go back home to England. From master he was now happy to serve, as loyal as a Nigerian, trusted by some, hounded by others, but proud to be associated with building a new Africa that had become the centre of interest for the world. He looked at all the young Africans who in his day were regarded by the British as rebels, and smiled. Now they had become leaders.

More and more people were drifting into the quarters of the Minister, until the whole place was packed. These people from his constituency had come to see the celebrations, and some of them now felt that the Minister's compound was the best refuge from the police and the confusion of the city. The Minister ordered his servants to serve them with beer and mineral drinks. 'I have to treat them well.' He moved among them, shaking hands, embracing them. They called him familiarly by name and slapped him on the back.

A man carrying a notebook pushed his way towards him. 'Another pressman!' moaned the Minister in a tone of boredom.

The reporter was in his twenties. His dress was unkempt. His face was oily with dirt. His trousers had never been cleaned in their lifetime, nor could anyone imagine how he regularly got into and out of them, if he ever did, they were so narrow at the ankles and knees.

'I represent the *West African Sensation*. Excuse me, sir. . . . What exactly is the present function of the Ministry of Consolation?'

The Minister turned to the group. 'Excuse me, ladies and gentlemen.' He spoke in an aside, confidentially. 'The Press is here, and if I don' answer the reporter tomorrow he will write another report entirely.' His followers laughed. 'Tha's how the Press used to form public opinion.' The laughter doubled in volume and the Minister took the young man to a quiet part of the compound. 'What do you want to know, Mr Pressman? You don' want to ask me embarrassing question?'

'Mr Minister, may I ask what exactly is the present function of the Ministry of Consolation?' repeated the journalist with pencil poised. 'Before independence it used to be——'

'Well . . . er . . . you know, this Ministry looks after all the people, you know . . . women, men, children, who have no home, no father, no mother, no husband, no nothing, as they say! . . . Hem! . . . We take them in and we console them or help them. . . .' He showed his teeth in the manner which the mirror had told him was most flattering. The photographer appeared and began focussing his camera. The Minister manœuvred the reporter till he was farthest from the camera.

'Actually,' said the Perennial Secretary, coming to the rescue, 'the Ministry was founded as a sympathetic gesture, a kind of Universal Aunt. It was felt that Nigerians —men, women, children—must have somewhere to run to in times of need. For instance, you might like to see the orphanage. This way! . . . All the children were taken in by the Abandoned Children Division of the Ministry. The Ministry looks after their accommodation, health, education and so on. All the orphans in the Minister's constituency are brought here, and also some from the Federation as a whole. Mr Minister, if I may I'd like to show the gentleman the orphanage. . . .'

'Go ahead. Don' keep the gentleman long! I'm sure he wants to get back to his paper and write his report.

Don' forget to use my picture: on the front page! Ask the photographer to give you some copies.'

The reporter nodded casually and sauntered after the Perennial Secretary.

The Minister sighed. 'Those pressmen! . . . They never let us rest one minute!'

He went back to the compound, where the drinking and the chattering were going on with increasing zest.

10

NIGHT had come over the city and at the police headquarters, where Wilson was herded with the others, the noise of the city came to them with the muffled din of a league-cup final.

The streets told of what had happened. Cyclists riding past the police station complained loudly of shattered glass and litter. Wilson looked round at the handcuffed and the bludgeoned, who stood in groups. He thought: *The police, look at them! Gloating. They have made arrests. Some are going to be commended. Some will win medals. Where do you really stand? You will shoot down your very own brothers. You are paid to obstruct even that which you yourselves believe. Where do you stand?*

A constable approached him. 'You wish to make a statement?'

Wilson said nothing. He took the piece of paper from the constable and began to write.

At about three p.m. today, myself, Kwame Amantu and all the leading members of the NMFAMS assembled in the park for the purpose of leading a peaceful demonstration.

He underlined the words 'peaceful demonstration'.

The reason for the demonstration was to remind Nigerian leaders of our desire for African Solidarity. That was the whole reason. We were determined to be peaceful and methodical about it. We had designed posters, we had made every arrangement for a peaceful demonstration.

When we set off, after I had addressed the gathering, again warning them to be peaceful, none of us even thought our actions would result in rioting, looting, raping, shooting and confusion. We marched very peacefully from the park to the Carter Bridge. We marched up Nnamdi Azikiwe Street and beyond Isalegangan, where we held our rally. There was nothing unusual in this. The rallying ground is open to all.

It was here that the main contingent from Northern Nigeria, Western Nigeria and Eastern Nigeria joined the demonstrators in Federal Nigeria. The Northerners rode horses and carried the placards on their long trumpets. Brother Jacob did a fine job rallying them together.

From Isalegangan, we marched towards the race-course, where the Independence Anniversary celebrations were going on. It was here that a police officer challenged us for the first time with the insulting words: DISPERSE, YOU REBELS!

We paid no heed to the police. It was here, too, that I saw a lorry-load of police officers, wearing steel helmets, being tumbled down. Their attitude was hostile. As soon as they got down, they formed themselves into line and made a baton charge on us. We were forced to stand and fight back, though unarmed.

Then they began firing tear-gas shells at us, and that broke us up. The orderly procession immediately became disorderly, and from that moment on the conduct of the demonstration was out of my hands.

It must be remembered that many of the people who later joined us were not necessarily organized and responsible members of the NMFAMS. Some of them were hooligans and unemployed, and I think the best thing to do would be first to fill these people's bellies before putting the blame on the NMFAMS. . . .

Wilson had been so absorbed in writing his statement that he had had little time to look up. He read it over to himself, chewing the end of his pencil. For one moment, out of habit, he looked at his watch and saw that it was the usual time when he called at the pharmacy. Today was a public holiday and the pharmacy must remain shut.

All this time a man had been trying hard to catch his eye. Wilson handed in his statement. The constable read it over, and said:

'You will follow me.'

Wilson followed him and walked along the gutters to the little cell at the back where they pushed him in for the night. He was bloody, but his head was unbowed.

Wilson gripped the iron bars of the cell door and looked at a world which did not in the least care about African and Malagasy Solidarity. Somewhere in all this mess there must be Nigerians who considered him a reactionary, a traitor in his own country. Of course, they did not understand him; never would. This was an age in which stagnant thinking must not be allowed to plunge the nation into a state of stupor and inactivity.

He heard footsteps, and a moment later there was a constable standing at the door of his cell. It was the same man who had locked him in.

'There he is,' he said.

A man came from behind the constable, flinging his trailing robes over his shoulder.

'Oh yes, you're right. That's him all right.'

The constable stood uncertain, and the man introduced himself. 'My name is Paul Aremu.'

Wilson looked at him closely. He had an air of wealth coupled with something of the intriguer. Wilson felt a slight unease due to no reason he could find.

'I have been very interested in your movements all along and now I have seen you're really anxious and ready to suffer for your convictions. That is commendable. I have come to reveal myself to you.'

Wilson looked at him cautiously.

'What's your proposal?'

'This is not a good place to talk.'

'You want to bail me out?'

'That's what I come for.'

Paul Aremu disappeared and when he reappeared he was waving a note in front of him. The jailer unlocked the gate and Wilson came out, once again breathing the air of freedom.

'I'm going to the hospital,' he said.

'I come with you,' Paul Aremu offered.

Wilson had never seen the emergency ward packed so full. He picked his way through the crowd and stood beside a white man down whose face the streams of blood had clotted.

'Iyari, Iyari!' came the call.

He could find neither Kwame Amantu nor Brother Jacob, but when he asked was told that Kwame had been admitted. He followed them along the corridors till they came to the accident ward.

The radio was saying something. He listened.

'In a statement issued earlier this evening the Minister of Consolation deplored the irresponsible action of the NMFAMS who were responsible for disrupting part of the Independence Celebrations in the capital city of Lagos. The Government advises all right-thinking Nigerians to go about their business in a peaceful manner. Nigeria has a name in the world for maturity, logical thinking and solidarity. The idea of being so emotionally flaunted by these conceited young men is not new to the country. We, as leaders who have your mandate, are already battling with the problems. The leader of the NMFAMS has been apprehended and will be given fair trial in accordance with the Constitution.'

'Wilson, that's you!' It was Kwame. He had crept up while they stood listening. He had a swollen eye.

'Have you seen the others?'

'Brother Jacob was arrested. Most of the others are here in the accident ward.'

'Oh, Kwame, I feel pleased. Now, whatever happens, we have brought our case to the notice of the authorities.'

'Mark my words. They are going to act on our ideas, but they will not give us credit. Who is the gentleman with you?'

'My name is Paul Aremu. I am very impressed by the orderly bearing of you gentlemen. I shall give you my full support.'

'You're welcome,' Kwame said, and they shook hands. 'Let's go now. I've had my treatment.'

The Cadillac was parked under an Indian almond tree. A group of ruffians had assembled and were examining it with interest.

'I bought it when I went to the States,' Paul Aremu said. The driver jumped out and opened the doors for the men. 'They're quite cheap in America.'

Wilson felt an overwhelming desire to see his home again, but even before they got out of the car he sensed the hollowness. His wife had not returned. The house was still empty. He smiled secretly. There was an amusing comment somewhere in all this. He was fighting for the solidarity of the whole continent, and his wife was fighting against him.

'I feel like . . . like a total stranger.' The words came out and the two men looked at him curiously and said nothing.

He went to the fridge and produced drinks.

Paul Aremu said: 'Where's your wife? Oh . . . wise man! If I were you I would do the same. No need exposing her. Very wise indeed. You know, I'm beginning to like you more.'

Paul Aremu toyed with his drink. Finally he came to the point. 'How much money do you need to run your party?'

Wilson said: 'We're not really a party, you know. We are just observers, sentinels of the people. Just like political newspaper columnists. We are interested in African Solidarity. We want Nigeria to bring about African Solidarity in all its forms, regardless of all difficulties. It is not going to be easy, and it is not going to be done in two hours. We must start now.'

Paul Aremu drank in silence. Wilson waited for him to speak. 'All the same, you have influence—especially with the right-thinking men.' He shook his two fists. 'Think what it means! You will be the leader of all Africa. That's something!' He sat on the edge of his chair. 'Listen, I am prepared to give you fifty thousand pounds. It's not much, but it will tide you over a few months till you have established. You can't go back now. That's what I'm telling you; and you can't survive without money.' He took out his cheque-book and spread it on his knee.

Wilson said: 'Wait. What are the conditions?'

'Conditions? Ha! . . . You're clever. I want a seat in the House at the next elections, and I want the Minister of Consolation out of the way.'

Wilson Iyari began to laugh. He laughed until the

breath caught in his throat and the laughter became a pain in the chest.

'Why you laugh?' Aremu asked.

Wilson said: 'You talk like an American.'

'Why?'

'It is Americans who see red in everything. And it is reds who see revolution in everything. We are not interested in revolutions. We are only trying to use pressure to bring people to our way of thinking. Africa must be united; that's all we care for.'

Paul Aremu shook his head. 'And I thought you were serious!'

'We are....' Wilson glanced at Kwame, who seemed to be motioning him not to continue the argument. 'But why do you want the Minister of Consolation out of the way? And why must it be an NMFAMS job?'

'Because he is spineless! He is not a man of God. We need men of God these days, believe it or not. He is standing neither here nor there, only where the money is, the personal profit. He does not place the interest of Nigeria first, as you of the NMFAMS do, but of his own private interests. He is vain, conceited, stupid, empty, illiterate, a thorough fool, but shrewd enough to take everyone in. He doesn't fool me!'

Paul Aremu had become heated during the course of his vituperations. Wilson looked at him and was full of pity for him.

He turned to Kwame. 'I really wish we could do something to help you. But violence is not in our line.'

'It was due to all that nonsense that he took my seat away from me at the last elections.'

'And now you want your revenge——'

'In a big way, too!'

Paul Aremu hesitated. He explained that as a big-business man he had very little time to devote to the task of liquidating his rival. He would much rather leave it to the NMFAMS. The fifty thousand pounds included the cost of establishing a small press, THE VOICE OF THE NMFAMS. If Wilson and his men were not interested he would take his proposition elsewhere.

While they talked, Wilson tried to picture the Minister rubbed out of the way by the hands of an NMFAMS agent. He shuddered. He saw instead the face of the girl Chini whom he had saved from being raped earlier that afternoon. He could not get her face out of his mind.

Long after Aremu had left, he and Kwame sat talking. Kwame suggested that Wilson immediately begin looking for Yaniya.

11

This house that had known the ringing cries of children was now empty. Wilson walked from one room to the other, for the first time alone in a home broken by sheer pride. None of the neighbours could tell him much. One talked of a taxi which came, of a suitcase and flasks and baby food being hastily thrust into the windows of the taxi while the children cried out: 'Papa, Papa!' Those who had seen did not understand that Yaniya was in fact running away from home. What a sorrowful thing to happen!

Without waiting to listen to their consolation, Wilson drove straight to the suburbs, to Brother Jacob's. The street had its usual air of a market-place after market-day: riotous. Leaves floating in the street, dogs feeding from open dustbins, puddles of water splashing as cars raced and children scampered to safety.

He saw ahead of him a girl hawker carrying bread, swinging her hips and arms with the loose elegance so typical of girl hawkers. Her hands paddled her slim body, her neck danced to keep the vanishing balance of the loaded tray on her head, while her bare toes gripped the undulations of the earth. At the same time she was crying out musically to buyers the qualities of her wonderful bread.

Brother Jacob lived in the house just ahead of the hawker. Wilson parked the car carefully, remembering that children were always being crushed in this street by impatient drivers.

He walked along the corridor till he came to Brother Jacob's room and knocked. While he waited an empty foreboding filled him. Yaniya vanished; left. The door opened slightly, and Agnes, her head in a scarf, looked at him. She wore jeans.

'Nobody in the house, only me,' she said.

'What about Brother Jacob?'

'I don' see him since the demonstration.'

Wilson drew the obvious conclusion. Yaniya must have gone to see her father. She was always talking of the forest near Benin, which had been her father's kingdom. She had become a Runaway Wife. How did the Highlife tune go? Unconsciously he hummed it to himself.

> *If you meet a Runaway Wife*
> *Don't marry her!*
> *You never know what she may do*
> *She'll run again.*

He used to dismiss the tune as something too distant to affect him. Now it sounded neither funny nor distant. The problem had come home to him, to the leader who was advocating the unity of a continent. The runaway wife was his own wife. The broken family was his own. The children deprived of paternal care were his own. It was no longer a laughing matter. Yaniya had run away and left him, taking Lum and Pandhit and Jomo with her. But why? What had happened to their little home to make it unwholesome and uncomfortable for her and the children?

Agnes shut the door and Wilson discovered that he had been standing in the corridor a little too long. Someone might begin to guess that something was amiss. He turned round and walked towards the car. A group of children ran from under it as he approached.

In the motor station Yaniya was feeling hot and uncomfortable. She sat on a stool in the shade with little Jomo in her arms and a feeding-bottle pressed to his lips. Pandhit held a loaf of bread and gazed at the bustling crowd of travellers, hawkers, porters, passengers. The journey had not yet commenced, and Lum, who was wearing miniature robes, was asking her questions about his father.

'Papa is not here yet,' she said with irritation.

'When will he come, Mama? Before we leave?'

'He will come soon.'

'But he has not come yet.'

'He'll come, Lum. Papa will come.'

'Good, Mama. And then we'll all go together. I do not want to go if he will not come.' He was silent for a moment, and then he gazed at her and said: 'But why are we not using his car? I don't like this lorry. It is too dirty.'

She said no more. With a napkin she wiped the lips of Jómo and held him up for wind. A man she thought she knew was coming nearer and Yaniya straightened her dark glasses and bent her head down. The man stopped, turned round and walked into the lorry park. This was no time to meet anyone who would go and tell Wilson her whereabouts. The man stopped, and turned round.

She tried to keep her mind on the children. *Let us move, let us move! When are we going to move? Oh, when? Let us move before all Lagos sees and identifies me, before Wilson's spies inform him and take me back to him!*

The lorry owners had been grouped under the bonnet of the lorry for some time. Their hands were greasy. Yaniya wondered what they were repairing. She looked, overcome with fear. What if the lorry foundered? Would she be able to look after the children on the way? Had she enough food, water, drugs? She had left home in a hurry, and now she could not go back.

She had told no one of her intention. Brother Jacob did not know. She had deliberately kept the secret to herself because she did not want Wilson to rush after her in his madness a few hours after she had left. Brother Jacob would not have the time, he was so involved in his intricate plans for making money. His big craze now was to make thousands of pounds out of a no-good politician called Paul Aremu, a known enemy of the Minister of Consolation. She had warned him to beware.

She went and stood by the group peering into the bonnet. 'Driver, what time will we go?'

'Now. Just now.'

'You sure the lorry's all right?'

'No trouble, madam. We only checkin'. We travel jus' now. No trouble at all. Whoside you goin'? Not Benin? Jus' now you reach your town.'

He swung the spanner and went back to the engine.

She was sorry she had already given him the fare and her things had been packed too far inside the body to be available now. They would make no end of trouble if she decided not to travel with them, and there was no guarantee that the next lorry would be in a neater shape or in better hands.

Her hopes soared when she heard the engine roar into life.

The lorry left the motor station when the sun had tipped over to the west. At Ibadan the crew spent one hour peering under the bonnet. They still had not less than two hundred miles to cover and already the lorry was showing signs of strain. The sun had set and this was the twilight hour, the brief period when the palm trees are silhouetted against the flaming sky. When they set out from Ibadan the fingers of the flame were already darkening. They had travelled for about an hour when the lorry uttered a series of explosive sounds and came to a stop. The passengers groaned.

The driver and his mechanics brought out a mat and spread it under the lorry and took out their tools from the tool-cases. The children were fast asleep. Inside the lorry it was uncomfortably hot. Yaniya got down, spread a mat on the floor and gathered the children round her. A cold wind descended. She felt again the skin on Lum's face. It was definitely hot. She thought nothing of it this time, but half an hour later it was hotter and she herself began to have a dizzy feeling.

She remembered that she had not eaten, neither had the children had a decent meal the whole day. Lum's temperature rose. She had to do something, and quickly. In her state of panic it seemed to her as if she were walking in a dream. Herself on a highway, with all her children and one of them taken suddenly ill, dying. No, not dying!

She stood in the middle of the road, waiting for a lift, and at last a Land Rover stopped a few yards away. She ran up and saw that the driver was a white woman. She was full of pity when she heard Yaniya's story and agreed to take her to Benin. Patiently she waited till the suitcase was extricated.

The drive seemed an endless succession of corners and bridges. At every turn Yaniya asked whether they had reached Benin. In Benin they found a private doctor's address, but he had already gone to bed and they woke him up. The white woman left Yaniya and urged her to take the greatest care. She would have stayed on, but she had to be up early the following morning, and her night stop was by the ferry some ninety miles away.

When Yaniya saw the face of Lum all her anger turned to fear. His face was ashen and his eyes fixed. She called him out by name and he looked back at her and said the only word which had crossed his lips since they left home: 'Papa.' Yaniya wrung her hands in agony and mumbled prayers. She could not sit on the chair which the doctor had given her while he worked. Her eyes were fixed on the face of the boy, and once she thought he gave her a smile. She waited, pacing the room, while the doctor took Lum into the surgery. After interminable hours he emerged.

Yaniya again felt the skin on Lum's face. He was much cooler now. He smiled the distant smile of the sick child who senses a new power in the very threat of his sickness. Yaniya kissed him and put a cloth over him. There was no question of their continuing their journey that night. She sat up all night, not sleeping for one moment.

When morning came she found a new hope. The worst was over and though Lum looked very pale, Yaniya felt he was free from danger. The doctor told her she could travel to see her father in his kingdom. She found a timber-lorry bound for the forest and chartered it. The children sat in front with the driver on the bald wooden seat. The road became narrower and narrower and finally ended. One of the labourers helped her with her suitcase and one child. She tied Jomo on her back and led Lum by the hand. They proceeded slowly.

Yaniya inhaled the damp scented air of the forest. In the distance she saw the roof-tops of the three huts that comprised the village of Ol' Man Forest, Emorwen. The camp was a little clearing in the forest. The forest stretched out territorial arms of acquisition, but Emorwen slashed them back, keeping his area clean and well defined. Built of mud and thatch, the three huts were like a discovery in the jungle. Yaniya's heart bounced with joy as she set eyes on them.

She broke into a trot, marvelling at the immense-girth trees that flung extensive and lazy arms over the clearing, dripping dew like sweat from a performing athlete. Silently the monkeys looked down, disturbed by the strangeness of the visitors. The squirrels chirped and scampered into the thickets.

She saw her father in front of the huts, carving a stick with a machete. He looked older now with his white head and wrinkled skin. This man could tell tall stories of his days of glory when the camp was a village and he was chief.

He turned now. 'Who am I seeing, my daughter Yaniya?'

'It is even I, Papa.'

'Ah, I am glad. You come in peace?'

'Yes, Father.' She put down Jomo, while Lum and Pandhit ran towards her and clung to her skirt, terrified of Ol' Man Forest.

'Where's your husband?'

'I left him in Lagos. I am tired.'

'Come on, come and salute Ol' Man Forest!' He stretched out both arms to the terrified children. 'Your father has never come here. What kind of a son-in-law have I got?'

'He will come one day, Papa.'

'Now,' said Emorwen, 'you sit down. Men, put down the loads. Sit down and drink some palm wine. It is fresh, from the trees. I tapped it myself and did not put too much water, like the one they sell to you in the town. Ha, ha!'

The driver and his men sat down and drank and talked. When they were leaving, Emorwen called the driver and gave him five yams tied together and crowned with the leg of an antelope.

'You have done well, men!'

'Ah, may you be blessed, may you be blessed.'

Yaniya watched the lorry till it turned a corner and was hidden by the massive trunk of a tree. That was her last link with the world outside. She felt at ease. Lagos, the NMFAMS, Gadson Salifas, Brother Jacob, all the worries and problems of Lagos, could never reach her in this fresh-scented forest. She was safe.

Lum recovered quickly. He played in the woods and ran from one hut to the other. Once Yaniya warned him about the three huts. She showed him the one that must never be entered, because it was the oracle hut of Ol' Man Forest, where he communed with the cosmic. She showed him the central one that served as a sitting-room where strangers were received and kola-nut split. She took him to the last one which Ol' Man Forest reserved for important visitors.

They played in the clearing and went to farm with their grandfather. They saw the grave where Yaniya's mother and the mother of Brother Jacob had been buried. It was home, the earth of motherland.

Lum's relapse began one evening. He had been playing in the afternoon and suddenly he complained of a headache. His temperature shot up, he was shivering. Ol' Man Forest squeezed the juice of a leaf into his eyes. The boy was delirious, calling 'Papa!' Yaniya took him in her arms and prayed and prayed. She was holding him when he took a sharp breath and his body relaxed. He became suddenly too heavy to carry.

Ol' Man Forest rushed up and peered into his face, then looked away. Yaniya was numb with disbelief. The boy had been playing only a few minutes before. He could not be dead. He could not be dead. He could not be . . . Not here, no one to bear witness. 'Lum, open your eyes, you are not dead. Lum! . . . I am going to fetch Papa. Papa is coming, open your eyes and see him!' Ol' Man Forest came, and gently took the boy from her arms.

In the morning they washed the dead boy and dressed him in his finest shirt, the best that Yaniya had brought in her race away from home. Ol' Man Forest dug a grave beside the grave of his first wife, Yaniya's mother. Yaniya was stone-cold with grief. She loved her father, and now she spilled over the contents of her grief, seeking comfort and understanding.

'My own fault. My own fault. I killed him.'

She should never have travelled so many miles away, never have run away from home with the children unprotected, unprepared against the hazards of travel. Lum was gone. Wilson's favourite son and heir.

'The doctor said I must never have any more children. That is what pains me. How shall I pay for the death of Lum?' She sat still, watching Ol' Man Forest construct a bamboo coffin. Was the boy truly dead?

By now Ol' Man Forest had known that her journey was an escape from the life in Lagos.

'You will go back to your husband and beg him. Try and be a good wife to him. Don't ever run away.'

'I can never go back again.'

'You must. It is your duty.'

She cried and cried. She wandered in the forest all day, listless. She stopped by the river and bathed Jomo and Pandhit. She fed them forest fruits that reminded her of her own childhood. She thought of Wilson Iyari, her husband. In this forest atmosphere his personality had become invested with a wholesomeness it had lacked when they were together in Lagos. To her he had become the man who had been wronged.

But she could never go back. What would she tell him? How would she ever remove the guilt-feeling? She would tell her father to go and beg him. She would tell Brother Jacob. But would Wilson listen? She had never promoted any friendly feelings between Brother Jacob and Wilson. Always he was borrowing money which he never hoped to repay. She had deliberately insulted his pride many times and Brother Jacob had done nothing to reprimand her. No, she would never go back.

She knew how Wilson badly wanted sons. Lum was their first, and he loved him best. He would want another son, and she could never give him his wish. Now he had the full reason to seek happiness outside. The family was broken.

She wandered back to the camp. Ol' Man Forest sat still and silent. She could see no sign of the coffin, but going towards her mother's grave she found the fresh mound of earth beside it and burst into tears.

'I shall go back to Benin and leave Pandhit and Jomo in care of my father's second wife. I shall return to Lagos and hide myself from Wilson. I cannot face him now. A life deserves a life, and until I pay for Lum's life with my own I shall never be happy. Never. Because I killed him. Wilson, you will be right if you kill me. Please punish me. Do not forgive me, ever!'

The old man said nothing. He shrugged his shoulders. He was an old man who knew the way women babbled when they were grieved. He had seen many things and though he was sorry, he was unshaken, because he was Ol' Man Forest, her father. Life's trials were still to come.

12

To Wilson it was a strange land and even more strange that his first visit here should be in pursuit of his own wife. Benin. He had heard about the city from Yaniya, and he knew it had a history of explorers and warfare, massacres and sieges, in the days when the white man was trying to colonize Nigeria. He knew that the Kingdom of Benin once stretched as far as Lagos, that chiefs from far and near paid homage to the Oba. When he arrived in the city its museum quality took him by surprise. Everyone seemed to be carving wood or modelling clay. The gates of the city wall were still there and a road took him to the palace.

The Oba, in his white robes and crown of coral beads, was holding court. He sat at the end of a long table and the two sides of the hall were lined by his followers, who came up and greeted him in a peculiar manner that caught the very soul of his power. A man took Wilson by the hand and sat him down. He went to speak to the Oba, then came back to Wilson.

'Come, the Oba will see you.'

Wilson stood before the Oba and mimicked the greeting successfully.

The Oba said, 'Who is the man you seek?'

'Emorwen, Ol' Man Forest. My wife has run there.'

There was a murmur. 'Eccentric old man! Is he not dead yet?'

They told him the story of his own father-in-law, how he had been a hot-head in his day, and how his stubbornness kept him still in the forest, a lone dweller. They then suggested he borrow a bicycle. The Oba gave him a guide and they journeyed for hours till they came to the forest abode. There were three huts in the clearing, one of which appeared to be the oracle hut. Ol' Man Forest came out of the central hut and shaded his eyes. He was grey, in a magnificient kind of way. He had grandeur.

'Come, my son. What seek you?'

He was looking direct at Wilson as he spoke.

'I seek my wife, your daughter.'

'Then you are Wilson Iyari. . . . Come into the house that we may talk.'

Wilson felt a keen sense of fear.

The old man said: 'You young people! To sacrifice an innocent child for your quarrels!'

'Sacrifice . . . innocent?'

'Yes, your son Lum died. He is buried here, beside his grandmother.'

A blackness descended before Wilson's vision. There was an abyss that yawned and he was enveloped in it. Lum, dead. Lum, dead.

'He died here. Your wife tried her best. Not her fault, my son. God said his time was up. After all the doctor did for him in Benin. But nothing. . . . It was beyond our powers. . . .'

Nothing he said or did made any sense. Wilson was enveloped in an abyss of grief and it was black madness. He was fired by a fury of vengeful hate, to kill Yaniya, to crush her with his hands. He was choking and could not speak.

'Oh yes, women! She is my daughter, but I say all you have to do is leave her to herself. Her conscience will kill her. You will see! You will say I told you. Her conscience will kill her. She will be so lonely in her crime that she will seek for consolation elsewhere, but it will haunt her, for she will find no glory in it because you have hidden your pain. Did she leave home to hurt you? Then defeat her. Show her it is sweet. No, don't ask about her when you get to Lagos. I know it is not easy. Leave her alone. Oh yes! She will still want to be your wife. It is the law. She is yours. What you have to do is, be patient. Women thrive on tenderness. Even though she is flirting outside, she will still want you to assure her that you value her more than anything. I know them, fickle things!'

Wilson looked at the grand old man. 'Take me to see the grave.'

'Is here, at the back.'

They went to the back of the oracle hut. It was there —a mound of red Benin earth. If he should dig now he would see his well-beloved son Lum lying cold, silent, cruel. Death was absolute. And all because of Yaniya's stupidity and carelessness.

'It was a waste, father-in-law. May his soul rest in peace.'

'Amen. Amen! . . . You young people. Your temper is too hot. Too hot! You will not go back to Benin or Lagos, my son. Not yet! You will spend the night here with me. Here, in the camp of Ol' Man Forest. You must stay with your father-in-law.'

. . . . . .

They sat up all night in honour of the dead boy. There were large kegs of palm wine which they drank, and as they drank they talked. From the neighbouring villages, some four miles by footpath, had come dancers and drummers on Emorwen's bidding. They played and sang and danced, for it was an occasion for sadness.

Wilson felt his soberness thawing, but his reason remained clear. He heard his own voice with a new sharp ring to it and a relentless curiosity behind it. Wilson asked Emorwen the question: 'Why do you thus remain in the bush?'

Emorwen pondered. He took a long drink from a gourd and wiped his lips. 'My son, you will not understand. This is my kingdom. Every man has his own kingdom. Here I am free. I have no problem. I am happy. I have land, I have food, I have water. I am free. When you have lived in the forest, my son, you will find something about it. It fills you with satisfaction. They say I am eccentric. He, he! . . . Have you heard that one? Some say I am mad. Yes, I know they say it. But it is they who are mad because they cannot understand! They and their noisy towns. God made this village. But man made the towns; artificial things. When I go to Benin I run back to this place. They have all tried to make me leave this place. They want me to be like themselves! I refuse, so they call me eccentric. He, he! Your wife Yaniya tried. Your in-laws Brother Jacob and Brother David, they have given me up. I don't mind. I am going to die happy here. This is my home. Eccentric. He, he! . . .'

He told Wilson of the days of glory of the camp. It had been a thriving community. There was a weekly market, to which people came from all over Benin province. There was a saw-mill, forest guards came to inspect the felling of the trees. They used to have a night market.

'Have you ever been to a night market? It is like going into a new world. You go to market, and everybody is carrying a small flame of light in a little pot with palm oil. There is the smell of burning palm oil, and the light comes from the ground; you see everybody looking attractive. . . . Oh, those were good times. Now it is all changed. I will tell you this: there is also dishonesty here in my village, though I live alone. Thieves come here—all the way from Sapele! They come forty miles to rob an old man. The dishonest people are all in the towns. . . .' He took a long drink and listened to the drumming.

'Son, have you ever heard of Obazek? He was a big man in Sapele, where they work timber. He was crazy with love for Yaniya. He was the man who wanted to marry her before you. But there was disappointment and she went to Lagos. She wrote me when you married, but you have never come here. You only come to see the grave of your son. . . .'

They drank.

'No, I do not want to go into the town. Tell them for me. I am Ol' Man Forest, Emorwen, and my kingdom is here. I want to live slow, for I am old. I do not want to hurry to my death.'

The dancers were tiring. The palm wine was slowly giving out. There was something in bush life which was a balm on wounds. Values were still what they had always been. Time was a partner, not an enemy. Wilson made a mental note of Emorwen's camp as a future refuge for his pains.

The light had begun to show in the sky when the drummers dispersed. Wilson crawled into the room

Emorwen had provided for him. There was a mat stretched out on a mound of earth. He crawled into it and fell asleep.

The one thought uppermost in his mind was to get to Lagos and find Yaniya, to ask the full details of Lum's death.

When he saw the first outskirts of the city, with its piles of firewood, filling stations, recovered accident vehicles, he thought what a poor impression the city made on visitors who were seeing it for the first time. Somewhere in this flat city Yaniya was in hiding. He was sure she could not confront him. Where were Pandhit and Jomo?

He called at the INDEPENDENCE PHARMACY. The accountant looked at him in surprise, for Wilson had not been there for a long time. Business was slack, the clerk told him. A white man carrying his sick child on his shoulders came in, followed by his wife, who led a blonde-haired little girl by the hand. Wilson attended to them personally and stood talking with them for a long while. He did not want to go home, but sat in his pharmacy, reading through his mail. He had a bath and went to drink beer at the Zapataya.

He found a corner table where he could read through his mail. One of the letters bore an unusual seal, and opening it he found it came from the Prime Minister. He read through it over and over, then folded it away. When he looked up there was Kwame.

Kwame sat down and ordered a beer.

'Wilson, I went to the pharmacy and was told you were back. How did it go?'

'Lum is dead. Remember the day we went to hospital with him?'

'So sorry. So sorry indeed. Where's Yaniya? Is she back with you?'

'Haven't seen her. I'll catch up with her, though.'

'Come on, man! You're not suggesting it is her fault.'

'She will have to explain to me.'

'Don't take it too hard, Wilson. Death is inevitable.'

'I agree. But waste is stupid. The boy would not have died but for the stupidity of Yaniya. Why did she have to run away? And take the children, involve them?'

'She was fed up, man. Listen, Wilson. You were living all alone, going to the pharmacy, running the NMFAMS. She was lonely. And the only answer to it——'

'Was to take the children and kill one of them.'

'Not so. Try to see her own side. Remember once we suggested forming a women's wing? What became of it? Nothing! Anyway, I'm sorry. But don't blame anyone. What will be will be, as the song goes.'

The pain remained. Wilson tried to drown it, to take his mind off it. Occasionally the words cut across everything he was doing: Lum, dead. Your boy. Lum is dead. He was looking steadily at Kwame and mouthing a question.

'Well, Wilson, the job of the movement has been done. I am thinking of going back to Ghana, as you know. By the way, have you seen the world Press reaction? We got some telegrams, you know.'

'Who from?'

'Everyone. All the African leaders, everyone. And you know the main thing they all want is Unity. All of them want it, in spite of their differences.'

Wilson felt a glow of pride. 'Ah, our mission is almost achieved. Tell me, Kwame. Did they get our point? Did they see that what we really meant to do was not to criticize anyone, or to take sides with anyone, but to show them: we want Unity?'

'Some did, some did not. The Western papers reported something different. They reported rioting, looting, breakdown of law and order. An American paper said it was a savage and barbarous demonstration inspired by communists!'

Wilson immediately remembered his encounter with Ken Johnson and laughed. 'I am not talking of the Western papers, I am talking of the African leaders.'

'They were happy.'

'Listen, Kwame. I've just got this letter from our Right Honourable Prime Minister. He wants me to come and see him. Do you think——'.

'I don't know what to think.'

'Did we break any law?'

'Not that I know of.'

'Were we subversive?'

'No.'

'What does he want me for?'

'Can't even guess. When are you seeing him?'

'Tomorrow at nine. I returned just in time.'

'I'll go with you and give you moral support.'

Kwame drank off his beer and together they set out for the empty house where Wilson lived.

13

THE Prime Minister's residence overlooked the lagoon. Kwame and Wilson parked the car and walked up to the gate. The policeman at the entrance fixed them with a stern look. Wilson drew himself up. He could feel the sweat running down his armpits. He wore national dress because he knew the Prime Minister had ruled that his Ministers should endeavour to promote the Nigerian way of life. National dress pleased him.

'I have to see the P.M. Here's the letter from him.'

The officer read it, saluted and waved Wilson on.

Wilson turned to Kwame. 'You'll wait for me? I'll not be long.'

An orderly showed him into a tastefully furnished lounge. At first Wilson did not notice the Prime Minister reclining self-effaced and barefooted on a *catifa*. He was reading the Koran. Seeing him at home, Wilson felt a warm admiration for the man. There is still a belief in God, he thought.

'Ah, Mr Iyari, you have come. Sit down. What will you have to drink?'

Wilson hesitated. He looked hard at the Prime Minister, trying to read the nuances in his relaxed posture, the humorous, cynical eyes. Could this be the preliminary to some devastating disclosure? He decided it was not.

'Beer, sir. Cold beer, sir.'

A spotlessly dressed servant brought the beer and Wilson helped himself. He took the first sip and with a handkerchief wiped his lips. He was sweating with anxiety, but the Prime Minister coolly had an orange drink poured for him. He took a long drink and lolled back on his divan.

'How goes the NMFAMS, Wilson Iyari?'

'I—I can't say, sir.'

'No doubt you are surprised to be invited to see me.'

'Yes, sir. Very, sir.'

'I have called you to speak with you and to ask for your help.'

'My help, sir?' Wilson sat forward. 'My help?'

'Yes, your help. Or do you think a Prime Minister does not need the help of his distinguished citizens? You see, Mr Iyari, I have been following your activities with interest. I have to, you know.' He smiled as Wilson looked surprised. 'And I ask myself the simple question: Now that you have had your demonstration, what next? States are not run by demonstration but by constant tedious work. Sometimes it can be very tedious, eh? It would be a pity to waste such a brilliant man.'

'Pardon me, sir. I am not trying to run the State.' Wilson tried to smile. 'All I was trying to do was awaken interest in the subject.'

'And you were right. We all feel the same as you do. It is merely a question of method. Nigeria has chosen the path of truth. And you, Wilson Iyari, are going to be useful now, instead of criticizing. I take it you are still a loyal Nigerian?'

'Yes, sir. I shall be willing to make my contribution in any way you want, sir!'

'Very good. You are really a nice fellow, if I may say so, Mr Iyari. When I read about you in the papers I ask myself what kind of a fellow is this Mr Iyari. Now I have found the answer.' He smiled. 'Now, I have decided to send you to Dakar. To find the right path. You will lead the Nigerian Delegation to a Conference on African Unity.'

Wilson looked sceptical. 'Sir, but——'

'It is an order. You will go and report back to me all your findings. Arrangements have already been made, and your instructions will be sent to you.'

Wilson could not follow all the Prime Minister was saying. The whole thing struck him as illogical and incredible. *Why me?* The words rushed to his lips, but he forced them back.

'Yes, sir. I will have to consult the NMFAMS. I'm sure they will not object, if it is an order.'

'It is an order from your Prime Minister.'

Wilson rose and saluted. 'I am highly honoured, sir.'

Kwame was speaking to a pretty girl who immediately walked away when Wilson approached. Wilson said nothing till they were a hundred yards down the road.

'Kwame, I don't like it. I have to go to Dakar; lead a delegation. You hear?'

'What for?'

'P.M. says in the interests of African Unity.'

Kwame braked the car so suddenly that Wilson was thrown forward. He looked hard at Wilson but did not say a word. He started the car again and drove on. Wilson recounted his interview with the Prime Minister, the dignity of the man, his calmness and composure and the fact that he was sure Wilson could make a contribution. What surprised him most was that there was not the faintest sign of a threat or a challenge. It was a genuine invitation to make a contribution.

'I must be mad, but I really want to go. I must go, to erase the impression that the NMFAMS is merely a trouble-making organization with no concrete ideas. After all, this is a practical problem.'

Kwame wheeled the car into the drive. 'I still have to think it over. It is a delicate matter, Wilson. Give me time.'

The next morning Kwame woke him up with copies of the daily papers. All of them had Wilson's picture on the front page.

Iyari to Lead Nigerian Delegation

REBEL LEADER TO MAKE CONTRIBUTION

IS THE NMFAMS DEAD?

Wilson smiled as he read the speculations, the bare-faced attacks. Much of it was uninformed. The journalists were writing from hearsay, from facts pilfered in the corridors of offices at ridiculous prices. One paper accused the Prime Minister of encouraging subversion. The right place for Wilson, the paper held, was behind bars. Another felt that Wilson had shouted so much that it would be interesting to see what he could do in concrete terms. Wilson wondered what the reaction of the Prime Minister would be, but he was new to the game and soon learnt that words written on newsprint were meant for wrapping bean-cakes by market women.

Overnight, Wilson found a new fame. Girls came to him. He could have them all, with their false faces and falser breasts bought in the department store. But none of the girls could smooth the ruffled nature of his inner harmony. He could send the NMFAMS van to pick them, any one of the glamourites who hung about the clubs and painted themselves, and they would be glad to come to his bed. That was what they really wanted. They were like a flock of bees, but unlike the bees they had no sense of direction. They floated with anyone who was riding high, they associated with headline makers so that some of the halo might shine on them. The pursed wet lips pressed against him in an artificial love-lust were not really honest. The sucking arms enveloped him in a web of selfish intrigue. He could not stand the infertility of the city women, their peeling make-up and blunt faces. He was tired of them and he told Kwame.

'They will tell you they believe in love, but you damned well know they don't. It's a lie; and they know you know. The poor brutes.' Wilson shook his head. 'Kwame, you got me wrong. Girls, yes. But happiness, no. It's an empty life without Yaniya.'

'But when Yaniya was here you were not on the best terms.'

'We had the children.'

'Ah, I see.' Kwame threw his *kente* over his shoulder. 'You mistrust everyone. I've noticed it. Since Yaniya left you have never been yourself. You are a strong man, but it broke you. What you are doing now is seeking a home outside. You cannot live without a home. Yaniya was your home. Do I sound like an old man?'

Wilson regarded him keenly. 'You sound like Emorwen, Ol' Man Forest.'

'Be serious. Yaniya is gone, bless her. She will not come back unless you show her sympathy. She has wronged you grievously. She is afraid of retribution. And you really need someone to comfort you. You have to think it over and decide. She is in Lagos, surely.'

Wilson was restless. Later in the evening he took the NMFAMS car and drove to the pharmacy. He entered through a door at the back and sat in his office working until the early hours.

14

WITHIN twenty-four hours the formal letter of invitation was delivered to him. For the next seven days Wilson worked in the Cabinet Office, shuffling papers, sending cables, dictating letters. A succession of smartly dressed secretaries wrote down his words, typed them out, cut stencils of them, fussed about him. And one morning she came to take his notes. He did not smile, he was so surprised.

'Chini?'

She sat down and crossed her sophisticated legs. 'I have been hiding from you. I knew you were here all the time.' He saw the mischievous smile on her face. 'I could not dare to come.'

'Hiding?'

'I did not want us to work together.'

'Why?'

'Nothing at all. . . . I just did not dare.'

For the first time he felt a self-consciousness. The old brusque manner, the distrust, broke down. For the first time he felt the need of woman.

'Where's your wife?'

'Gone. . . . Left me.'

'I'm sorry.' She shifted in her seat, taking a full deep breath. 'What about the children?'

'I don't know, I don't know at all! She may have taken them to her mother.'

'Wilson, I have not met your wife . . . but people who know her say that they see her often, here in Lagos. In the house of the Minister of Consolation.'

Wilson smiled. 'Perhaps she is seeking consolation.'

Chini laughed at that. 'You are funny, Wilson! Seeking consolation?'

'Well, what will a woman want with a Minister of Consolation?'

Chini held her sides and laughed. She took out a dainty handkerchief and dabbed her eyes. With pen efficiently poised over notebook, she looked at him. 'You were dictating something, sir . . .'

Her attitude pulled him up sharply.

'Yes, I was saying . . . I was dictating a letter to the President. . . . Take it down now. The problem of African Unity and Solidarity . . . is one which engages the attention of all right-thinking leaders in our great continent today. . . . It is a problem which is equally important to the small State as well as to the large one. . . .'

At the end of the dictation Chini rose and Wilson looked her over. She could easily pass for a model. While his own wife was stately and imposing, Chini was finely chiselled and as modern as they came.

'I shall be taking a secretary with me to the conference in Dakar. It's a very nice place indeed, so I hear, although a bit expensive. Have you ever been there?'

'No, Wilson.'

She turned and walked smartly to the door. While trying to open it her pen dropped and she bent down to pick it up. The charming way in which she bent over and smiled at him left in him a longing for her.

Yaniya had been waiting in the outer office of the Ministry of Consolation for some time. She was prepared to wait. The door into Gadson's office opened and closed. The last man came out, carrying a sheaf of files.

Yaniya slipped in. She saw the surprise on the face of the Senior Assistant Secretary.

'Ah-ah! . . . Who is this?'

She smiled. 'Are you surprised? Gadson, I must see you this evening. It is urgent.'

'What is wrong? Why are you acting like this?'

'Like what? Are you imagining things?'

'You look nervous, my dear. Well?'

She tore a piece of paper from his notebook and scribbled down an address. 'I am staying with a friend. The place is not easy to find. . . . Here!'

She turned to go.

'Yaniya,' said Gadson, 'not even a kiss?'

'Here in public?' She blew him one. 'Till I see you in the evening.'

She went straight back home and remained indoors until evening, when she came out and sat on the balcony overlooking the street. Her friend had gone out with a man, and her eyes were fixed on all cars that drove towards the end of the road with its pools of stagnant water and turgid drains. Two years ago not one house was put up in this part of the city, but now it was thriving. Lagos was indeed expanding, outwards and upwards. From the balcony she heard the sound of the machines from the neighbouring factory, rhythmic, productive.

She heard above it the voice of someone asking about the room where Mrs Wilson lived. It was Gadson.

'Yaniya, I left the car up the road.'

'You are being cautious. Welcome.'

She opened the door. There was one large bed in the room, and at the corner a small table with a chair. From the railings of the bed hung frocks, head-ties, wrappers. She sat on the bed, Yaniya the magnificent.

'I have come back to Lagos, Gadson. You did not even bother to ask about me.' Her breasts swelled. She folded her hands and held them between her thighs.

'I am sorry. I asked about you, but you know—your husband Wilson is so very jealous. And he has lots of spies, and thugs. . . .'

'Are you afraid? No need for that. I have left him— for good—I am tired of the life of loneliness and cruelty.' She pursed her lips and made eyes.

'Going to get a divorce?'

'It will be too scandalous. I am not going back to him, that's all.'

'What really happened?'

'It was all my fault. . . . You know we have not been getting on very well. So I decided to leave him, and take the children with me. I was fed up. It was during that demonstration of the NMFAMS.'

Gadson crossed his legs. 'Was that not a cruel thing to do? Deserting a man when he needs you most?'

'What could I do? If I told him he would not agree. I did not mean it to be cruel. I only wanted to escape. After all, in some way, I love him. I would not have married him if I did not love him. But he is so proud and he thinks only of himself. I am proud too, and both of us are stubborn. So we had to split. I love my children very much, Gadson. I took them with me, and unfortunately one of them died.'

He sat forward, shocked. 'Which one?'

'The eldest, Lum.'

'Oh, dear! . . . The one Wilson loved best of all!'

Tears came to her eyes. 'I can never forgive myself. I tried, but could do nothing to save him.'

Gadson's car keys fell from his grasp and he let them lie on the floor. 'May his soul rest in peace.'

She took a handkerchief from inside her brassière and wiped her eyes. 'I don't want to remember it, Gadson. And it is my only fear. I feel I owe Wilson a life. He loved the boy too much. Too much. It will kill him when he knows of it. And, you see, I would have gone back to him, but the doctor said I cannot have any more babies. I nearly died when I was having Jomo. How can I repay him?'

Gadson was staring at her legs. He cleared his throat.

'You are not listening, Gadson! . . .'

'I—I am. . . . Yes, honestly, I do not know how you can repay him. Repay him? Do you believe in a life for a life?'

'He was a small boy, but he was a life, Gadson. Wilson loved him more than his own life. I am not afraid what he may do to me. I am only fearing how I can repay him for the loss. I remember the night you and I were out together. When I came back to the house he and his Ghanaian friend Kwame had taken Lum to the hospital. Lum had a sudden attack, you see. And I was just coming from you! I felt so wretched. A careless mother. Wilson did not talk to me any more from that night. I could not stay under the same roof again, so I packed away.'

'He suspected you?'

'I am sure of it. After that night he changed.' Her eyes narrowed. 'I was not afraid of him all the time, until that night. I knew he could kill me if he had the chance. He became cold. Do you know what it is to stay with someone who is cold, really cold, towards you? I decided to leave. . . . I should have known then the risk I was taking, but I did not care. I loved you, but you kept on following other women.' She saw the smooth smile on his face. He opened his lips but she carried on, not listening. 'What could I do? I could not turn to you. . . . So I went to my father, the old man who lives in the forest.'

'I'm so sorry. Where's your brother?' Gadson rose and sat beside her on the bed. 'Can I do anything?' He held her hands, but she shook him off.

'You are a Senior Assistant Secretary in the Ministry of Consolation. Please introduce me to the Minister of Consolation. I beg you. If you really love me I know you will do it.'

Gadson jumped away from the bed. 'Are you crazy? What do you want that for?'

'I want him to help me become an air hostess. I hear they are taking girls, and he has the influence.'

'An air hostess, but why?'

'Because it is a dangerous job. My plane will crash, and when I die Lum's life will have been avenged.'

Gadson began to laugh. He laughed and rolled on the bed, holding his sides. 'This is the stupidest thing I ever heard. Do you think a plane is more dangerous than a car? You're mistaken, my dear. If you really want to die think of something else. Or could it be that you prefer glamour? Anyway, I do not know the Minister well enough to introduce you or to ask him favours.'

'Say you do not want to help me, that's all. I knew it

would be like that.' Her voice had a ring of disappointment.

'No, not that! You see . . .'

'I know why you do not want to help me. You have other women. You have never really loved me. All you wanted was my body, that's all. Anyway, it is over now. I loved you, I was loyal to you. I kept your secret. I behaved to you with complete respect. And now I ask you something, a simple thing, and you refuse.' She was sobbing. Gadson put an arm round her.

'You don't want me to be sacked, do you?'

She cleaned her eyes. 'All you think of is yourself, your job, your promotion, your future. Leave me alone, selfish man!'

He picked up his keys and made for the door. He went down the stairs and she called him back, but he was walking out of her life now that she was 'free'. He was one of those men who liked other men to bear the burden while they enjoyed the fruits. He was shallow, pleasure-seeking, spineless. Now that Yaniya was alone, the thrill, the adventure of stealing her from her husband, had vanished. She would constitute a responsibility which he was not prepared to carry. Yaniya felt more alone than ever.

'I shall get there, Gadson! . . . You will be here in Lagos and see with your eyes.'

Gadson guided his car among the hawkers, cyclists, taxi drivers, bus passengers, cars which drove straight at his own, intent on ramming him, pedestrians who paid their tax and therefore defied any motorist to knock them down on the highway. A hundred yards down the road he parked the car near the petrol station and walked across the market to the tall house with the four floors and one hundred rooms. The woman whose charms he sought lived on the third floor.

He mounted the steps with a sure foot, knowing that her husband was still in jail, and would be there for another eight months. He had met her casually one afternoon, offering her a lift in his car, but not stopping when he had taken her home. Something about her reminded him of Yaniya. She was as tall and stately, as glamorous and fair. With her husband away in jail, Gadson found that she was in need. He had promised her work, but she was a fast one and was always away until late in the night. He held his breath and prayed for luck. Standing opposite the door of her room, he looked down the corridor and saw the other tenants, some watching their cooking, others eating, the majority just loafing.

He knocked and a female voice answered. She was inside. He pushed open the door. She lay on the bed, half covered by a transparent cloth. The curtains were drawn and the room smelt of sweat and warm groundnut stew. She pulled the cloth quickly over her breast. Gadson walked across, trying to accustom his eyes to the light. He put a hand on her hips. She stared at him sleepily and held his hand.

'How are you, sir? Ah, I am so tired. . . . Did I leave the door open? . . .'

'Oh, I forgot. . . . Let me just close it. I've called here several times, but you are always out.'

'So sorry, sir. What about the job you promised me? Can I start tomorrow?'

'Just a minute, there are complications. I shall explain.' He went to the door to shut it. His tie was already slackened and his heart was pounding harder.

At first he did not connect the presence of the men he found at the door with his own presence in the room of another man's wife, a man who was languishing in jail. But he saw now that the men were staring at him, and menacingly too.

He smelt the thick smell of beer mixed with palm wine and knew the men had been drinking.

'Tha's him,' said one. He was very dark and wore a beard.

'Useless man, you call yourself Senior Service. When a man go to jail you come and sleep his wife.'

'We must flog him till he get sense today.' He pulled out a rawhide whip, a *koboko*. 'You don' know say she be somebody wife? Our friend wife? Or you no get your own wife. If you go to jail will you like somebody to come and sleep your wife?'

Gadson could only stare back. He stood rooted with feet heavier than the Independence Building. Run, shout, beg? What would be best? Bluff his way out of the tight situation? He heard the voice of the woman he had come to seduce, thin and weak, begging for mercy. 'Leave him alone, he's my cousin. . . . He's helping me. Leave the gentleman. . . .'

It was too late. They pulled him out of the room and into the corridor. His back cracked under their merciless thrashing. His shirt was in tatters and his skin lacerated with large weals.

'Next time when you see another man wife, you go be careful. Damn' fool, Senior Service!'

They kicked him down the steps and he crawled along the street till he found his car. He tried to start it, then noticed that two of the tyres away from the traffic side of the street had been stolen and the car supported on stone blocks. He dared not walk home in this condition or enter a bus. He could not return to Yaniya because she would not have him. He hailed a taxi and bent his head and mumbled something about driving fast.

Amid boos the taxi drove him to a private hospital. Gadson quickly invented a tale, and was uneasy till a bed was assigned to him.

15

WILSON had tried in vain to trace his wife in Lagos and now he was leaving for the conference. At the airport he noticed the girl in the white blouse, tight blue skirt and rakish beret as his car stopped. The girl's legs were elegant and her height arresting. He saw her from the back, shapely and evocative, and he was sure he had seen her before. Then she turned and he recognized Yaniya, his wife. He stared at her and she stared at him and for a moment she could not move.

As he came out of the car she walked into the arrival and departure shed and he did not see her again until later on when he was too engrossed in checking the baggage to speak with her. In any case, was this the place to start discussing the death of Lum? There was absolutely no time. He saw Chini talking with her and wondered where they met. His plane was due to leave in a matter of minutes, so the loudspeaker said. He cleared the luggage through the Customs, checked his health and immigration papers and was through.

'Chini!' he called, 'you'll be late. . . .'

'Coming!' She bade goodbye to Yaniya.

Wilson watched them with increasing jealousy and irritation.

He thought of Lum and became immediately sad.

Why did he have to see Yaniya now? This was no time to remind him that he was fighting for the unity of people he did not know, for a reason he believed was genuine, yet he was alone.

He pictured what always happened when he dressed up and appeared in public and they waved greetings at him or cheered him in his car. Little did they know. He was a hollow man. He had no money. No roots. Yaniya had become the poisoned arrow in the wound. Pull her out and the flesh came away, leave her in and the wound festered and killed. The family had disintegrated.

All through the plane journey he lay on his back in a kind of stupor. It was a special plane and he had memories of the elegant air hostess who kept changing her frock at every stop—there must have been ten stops at least—between Lagos and Dakar. Every hour the plane stopped, and every hour the air hostess came to offer him something to soothe away his air-sickness. For the third time he went to the toilet and retched, and he came back and lay on his back. Chini placed a wet handkerchief across his brow and the scent and musty air choked him to exhaustion.

He tried not to think of the conference. He folded away the file on his knee and slipped it into the brief-case which Chini kept under her custody. Men drifted about the plane, black men in light-weight suits who spoke French, American, English, Somali, Yoruba, Hausa. Wilson tried to classify them. Those who spoke French he immediately classified as coming from the ex-French territories. The American-accented ones must come from Liberia, and the African language and English ones from other parts of Africa. He lay on his back, not moving. The air hostess was again smiling at him. She must be

Lebanese. Africa must run all her own airlines, Wilson thought. More and more.

The plane lost height suddenly, banked, and his stomach heaved. He saw Dakar beneath him, towers and match-box-shaped houses and the sea, a motor-boat streaking along beneath them. . . . Then there was a rumbling of engines. . . . They had landed. The air hostess stood at the door.

The small crowd of men inside the plane began to gather their belongings. Wilson looked through the window of the plane. He could recognize the Nigerian residents in robes and colourful hats. As soon as he descended, the group came towards him, the leader dangling a cigarette from his mouth.

'Welcome . . . have you had a good flight? Welcome.'

Wilson looked about him and immediately the burning hope of Africa was here evident. These men were all black and they carried brief-cases and looked as if the future of the world was tucked away under their armpits. Brotherly love glowed on their faces, and patriotism, loyalty and, above all . . . fight. African Solidarity. African Unity. Wilson heard the phrase over and over. African Solidarity. Something in their attitude spoke to him.

It seemed to say: *We are here to live, to find ways, to seek for truth. No blind decisions. We are here, like the morning light, to shine our mark on everything.*

Still he had that dizzy feeling. He looked round instinctively for the air hostess who had doctored him, but she seemed not to know him any more, passing by him without so much as a smile, her hands linked with those of a white man wearing soldier's uniform, her footsteps pointing towards the pavilion. Obviously her responsibility for him, her courtesy and friendliness, did not extend beyond the wing-span of the plane.

Chini came and took his arm and together they went to the waiting hotel omnibus.

Wilson walked towards the Independence Square in Dakar, his brief-case tucked under his arm, and Chini by his side. It was the day of the Plenary Session, and the city had come out in its full colours.

'Taxi, m'sieur!' they hailed from the Square, while buses unloaded passengers and touts sold dud watches and camphorated cigarettes.

At the entrance to the Ministry he stopped to admire the guards in their musketeers' red cloaks, scarlet drapings and shiny black skins. They reminded him of some weird dream, and when the black men in the jet-black Citroens began to arrive he was afraid. This was a strange process in reverse, and yet the Africans were taking it all normally.

And then the Nigerian Minister of Conferences was there and they were talking tactics. A guard broke into the discussions and told them they were awaited. The Minister of Conferences spoke a little more and they all rose and walked along the marble floor towards the conference room.

The room was dark with black men in black suits and black expressions on their faces. Cigarette smoke hung in the air, and coiled within it was a spirit of intense expectancy which immediately communicated itself to him. Flashes of light illuminated transiently this important room as some cameraman took pictures.

Wilson looked for Chini and found her already seated at the secretarial desk with earphones smartly clipped on, waiting for the conference to begin. There she sat at the horseshoe-shaped table, smart, up-to-date, decorative and functional. Her pen glided over the paper, but her eyes had been fixed on his face for some time. He was proud of her superb grooming. The extra yards of delicate Nigerian costume floating over her arm added a touch of honesty towards things African.

16

WILSON relaxed in his hotel room with the conference papers before him. He had read over and over the briefs and the secret instructions, and now his mind wandered over the strangeness of it. Alone in his room he asked himself: Was Unity necessary at all, or was it not? And if necessary, was it possible? He saw now the sleepless nights which the great leader must spend, trying to find an answer to the problem? So far, he had been very surprised at how smoothly everything went.

In the street below, the noise of cars stopping and starting again, the hawkers selling cigarettes, the laughter of girls clad in the flimsiest of nylon material and stiletto heels, all had become a familiar feature of his first seven days in the strange city. This was a city where a man's virility was taxed to the utmost. It was a city where fashion was the goddess and a man could stand at a junction and believe that all the girls had just stepped out of the Champs-Elysées and were on their way to a cocktail party with the President. Where did they find the money to pay for their fashion-consciousness?

He heard the gentle knock, but was not sure and listened again. He opened the door and Chini brushed against him into the room. There was nowhere else to sit, so she sat on the bed.

'Not going out?'

'No, just reading and thinking.'

'About your wife?'

'About Dakar, at first. . . .'

'You were watching us at the airport in Lagos, myself and Yaniya. You wanted to know what we were talking about.' She heaved her big breasts. Her lips were painted a startling red and a chain of Dakar beads graced her neck. She must have been shopping at lunchtime on Avenue William Ponty.

Wilson noticed also that she now had a new hairdo. Overnight, Chini the Nigerian girl had been transformed into a Senegalese. The very tight dress she wore was zipped at the back and cut very low in front. For the first time Wilson saw her as a female, with cool velvet legs and kissable lips, a young and slim girl.

'What were you talking about? I mean, with my wife at Lagos?'

'D'you know that was the first time I really knew she was your wife. . . . I've never seen you both together. I met your wife at a sewing class. She was much liked. I didn't attend long enough. When I saw her in air-hostess uniform I was trying to find out what had happened, and she said she had left her husband, and there you were. Anyway, Wilson, I think you should take her back. She told me how your son died, how she feels guilty . . .'

'Guilty, eh?'

'So she said; and that's why she took on a job as an air hostess. She thinks it is dangerous. And, again, it will make her get away from the world she knows.'

Wilson smiled. 'I don't think it is something we can lightly make up. I loved her, but it is over now. We are still friends. Only we are not compatible.'

'I know you still love her; it shows in everything you do.'

'Was that what you came to tell me?'

'No, I came to tell you to be kind to her. Forgive her. Come, Wilson. Forget your problems for a while. Let's go to the Ballets Africaine. Let's go to the Théâtre de Palais. See the people, study the language.'

'In ten days?'

'It's possible.'

'No, what I am interested in is the big hunt we are trying to organize.'

'Tell me about it.'

'There's nothing, Chini. You see, someone said that there is plenty of game in the hinterland of Senegal. During the week-end some of the delegates will be taken by guides —white men—into the bush, and they will shoot. Just for sport.'

She sat up, her eyes wide open. 'Don't go, Wilson. You sit here! The P.M. did not send you here to go and shoot antelopes. It's dangerous.'

'It's too late. I've already given my name.'

'Please don't! For my sake.' She half stood up, and Wilson stared at her. The soft light, concealed, moulded her lovely figure.

'I remember when we first met, Chini . . . near the INDEPENDENCE PHARMACY. You came out of the traffic and challenged me.'

'You were quite nice to me. I was a nuisance. I feel ashamed of my action now. But you were so famous . . .'

'I admired your guts, Chini. But I've never really seen you as a woman until now.'

He tapped the side of the bed. 'Come and sit by me.'

She hesitated, then sat on the bed, but not near enough to warm him. He could sense the rise and fall of her breasts and fill his senses with her French perfume. Softly he touched her fingers. She was breathing quickly. She looked at him out of the corners of her eyes, mute appeal blended with a warning of danger.

'Be a good boy, Wilson. Your wife is my friend. Please!'

He was deaf.

'It's not funny. I feel so guilty. I did not come here for that. We are not in our own country. How we behave matters. Wilson——'

'Chini, don't make excuses.'

'I was a fool to come here. I'm sure. It was all my own fault. I should have known. But I was bored.'

'You did right. But I want you. I have always wanted you. Don't make excuses.'

She sighed. 'Please, Wilson!'

He pulled her firmly but gently. Then he saw the tears in her eyes. A sudden tenderness overcame him. He kissed her full on the lips. She was silent, uncoiling like a snake in his arms.

'What are you going to tell your wife? She was my teacher at the sewing class.'

'There's nothing to tell. Yaniya killed my child and left me. Has she ever come to beg for mercy?'

'I'm sorry.' She stroked his forehead. 'Wilson, you worry too much and work too hard. You are too lonely, you keep too much to yourself. You need someone, you need a family, a home . . .'

'Perhaps. But what kind of a woman would suit me? I have no patience with those who think that sophistication is lipstick, high heels and fast driving. Give me a woman behind me or beside me always. Not one who runs away in my hour of greatest trial! Yaniya ran away when

I was leading the demonstration. That's why they say I am nothing but beautiful feathers.'

'I don't understand.'

'Well,' Wilson sighed, 'there is an Ibo proverb which says that a white fowl is beautiful only in its feathers. Once plucked, you are left with something commonplace. You see? As for me, I don't think I am capable of really loving anyone now.'

'But you are so gentle. I never could have thought so.'

'I cannot keep women because I think only of two things: my pharmacy and the Solidarity of African States. One is my profession and the other is my hobby. But the hobby seems to be getting the better hand. And there is little time to look into the face of my wife.'

'Everyone needs a happy home life, Wilson. Without that we all suffer.'

'Who doesn't, Chini? Sometimes I think the greatest happiness is in death. A dead man does not worry, only the living do.'

'You're cynical.'

'Tell me about yourself.'

Chini said: 'There's nothing to tell. I was married at eighteen and when in hospital my husband took up with another woman, older than myself and more experienced in the ways of life. When I came out we parted. I suffered a lot. That's all. My father refunded the dowry and I was free but shamed. Now the elderly woman is proving childless, see?'

'You made headlines once. What was the real truth?'

'I was in love, but that is a long time ago. It will not interest you.'

'Francis Garret was the name of the man. I remember reading about him.'

She leaned back and crossed her hands over her knees. 'An Englishman.' Her voice became softer. 'A man of fifty-five, due to retire. I was only twenty-two then. I have his child. We call him Babatunde. I loved Francis, he was so tender and understanding, but he had to go. You know all this to-do about Nigerianization. Well, when he left I could not understand it. I asked myself what is this stubborn, obstinate, implacable body of abstract creatures they call the Government? I knew them as people, but when they come together it is a different thing. Whatever hath been written shall remain. They took a stand against him, and that was that. The God-men must be satisfied, so he had to go.'

Wilson saw the mist in her eyes. She was very bitter. She burst out: 'You know what pained me most? They made capital out of it in the newspapers. They interviewed him and wrote articles, but the day he was to leave no one came to the wharf to see him off. The noise had died down and the newspaper editors were shouting about the new tax increases. There was a short article attacking the award of new contracts to a French firm instead of to a Nigerian. And my boy was going away—for good, and against his will. Francis, my love!'

She began to weep now and Wilson put his arm round her and held those breasts overripe for love, firm and sophisticated in their cups.

He could see the parting scene clearly as she talked.

Francis Garret, the Englishman, waving at the country he loved. The milling crowd, noisy, but no one for him except Chini. Twenty-odd years of his life behind him. Francis saying to Chini: 'I can't believe it. I just can't believe I'm going back. I'd like to stay, but it would embarrass everybody. . . .' The boat heaving as passengers climbed in and cranes swung the heavy loads. Chini holding little Babatunde in her arms, the image of his father with brown eyes, fuzzy blonde hair.

'I suppose . . . there's something typically Nigerian in all this. . . .' The words of a departing man.

'I don't know, Francis. I don't know.'

The boy, whimpering. Chini taking him down below for a moment with his father, then leaving with Babatunde in her arms. Francis Garret staring with eyes blurred, watching the beating surf, the waving fronds and the retreating coconut palms. In two years from now he would come back if he could, and would never be able to identify it all. In a decade he would neither recognize his own son, nor know him, the country changed so very fast.

Wilson kissed away her tears. 'Chini, it is always like that. A man gives his life to Africa. He makes a little mistake, he goes, but his heart remains. It is not every white man who takes his soul with him. . . .'

Chini placed her head on his shoulders and sobbed till the drowsiness stole over her. Wilson smoothed back her dress and placed a cloth over her feet. He had wanted her as a lover, but now he thought of her as a sister.

At the week-end the hunting party set out for the game fields outside Dakar. Wilson led the Nigerian team and from other parts of Africa very important people formed the team. Americans, Russians, British and French observers brought up the rear—as gun-bearers. Wilson saw now that things were working in reverse. The black man could hold his head high: one of the many joys of Independence, reversing the course of history.

The white men did not complain, but were silent, and

no one suspected anything. Occasionally they met and whispered among themselves or laughed. Wilson called aside a delegate and tried to tell him: 'Look, the world is watching and listening. We must behave our best!'

'*Non compres pas!*'

The delegate shrugged his shoulders and walked off into the woods, and at that moment a huge beast shaped like a rhino, but infinitely more elegant, came charging down towards them. Wilson fired, but he also heard the sound of other shots, three or four—before the beast stumbled, leaving a trail of blood, shattered shrubs and indistinct footprints which they followed till they came to the riverside.

Wilson was among the first to reach the dead beast. It was a very rare specimen and no one could name it, but everyone believed it was highly prized. Some of the hunters wanted the horns, some wanted the whole beast preserved in a museum, and immediately an argument arose and voices become loud. Nobody knew who squeezed a trigger. There was the sharp crack of a shot and everyone ran for cover. Confusion spread.

Wilson saw the white men carrying off the beast and running down the slope. He aimed at the retreating white men, but a shot struck him in the ribs and he fell. He lay there in a shot-riddled mist, choking for breath, while his body floated in endless circles, weightless.

Wilson opened his eyes and saw standing by his bed a female nurse, attentive, listening. He identified the seated man as the President.

'I do not speak much English. You will pardon me, M'sieur Wilson.'

Wilson was charmed.

'I speak no French at all, M'sieur le President.'

'I have heard what happened when you went shooting in the bush. It was for sport, yes?'

'For sport, Excellency!'

The President shook his head sadly. 'You know . . . it is like the struggle for African Unity. While Africa burns, interested parties carry away the loot. We must be on our guard, must be ready to give and take. . . .'

Wilson stole a glance at the President's face and was startled at the transformation. His features glowed with a new light.

Wilson tried to shift in his bed and found that he was strapped down. He felt a flash of anger and lay back. After a time the President, who had been talking for a while, seemed to have come out of his trance.

'I'm sorry, M'sieur Wilson. I forgot myself. But the problem is always with us.'

He motioned and an orderly in scarlet uniform came in and handed over a velvet-lined case to him. It contained an insignia of honour.

'This for your efforts, M'sieur Iyari.' He pinned the glittering object on Wilson's shirt and shook him by the hand. Wilson saluted as best he could.

The President rose, and, preceded by his troupe, walked down the hospital hall. At that moment Wilson's heart was full of joy. He looked up and saw Chini standing now by the bed and gazing at him with reverent eyes.

To Wilson it seemed as if his Prime Minister had not moved one inch since he saw him last. He had been away for two months, not ten days, as planned, and now he was back in Lagos and the Prime Minister was lying back on the couch, relaxed and smiling.

Wilson saw the twinkle in the great man's eyes and was uneasy. It could not be mockery. It seemed to say, 'I told you,' and yet it was not jubilant.

With his Koran the Prime Minister pointed to the plaster and said, 'Feeling better, now?'

'A little, sir. I hope I shall be able to use the hand again.'

'Sit down. What will you have to drink?'

'Cold beer, sir.'

The spotless servant appeared. The Prime Minister watched while the beer was poured for Wilson, then ordered an orange drink. When he had sipped it he sighed.

'Well?'

'I have come to report to you as ordered, sir. Hem! ... The conference went quite well, sir. We were in agreement over the main points on the agenda. It was when we came to sport, when we wanted to relax ...'

Briefly, he recounted the hunting episode, culminating in shooting and looting by white men.

The Prime Minister listened patiently.

'My dear Mr Iyari. You are a young man.' His voice fell one octave. 'A very young man, and therefore impatient. You led a strike here because you thought Nigeria was this, Nigeria was that. Now you've seen for yourself how a very little thing can upset unity. But we must keep trying.'

'It was surprising, sir. I couldn't understand it.'

'It's human nature. I mean, you all began shooting at one another. Friends! Did you go there to shoot at one another or to shake hands?'

Wilson was silent.

'I have a letter from the President of Senegal and he speaks highly of you. Indeed he does. So, you see, that's something achieved.'

'It's something, sir. The President is a great man.'

'And now, I expect, you will want to go back and see your family. At least there is unity there.'

Wilson stared at him absently. 'Oh yes, there is.' He rose and bowed, inwardly afraid. He determined never to take part in the strenuous, argumentative process, the gives and takes, the ceaseless jockeying for position, that were involved in trying to please everyone. It was far easier to be a critic, a rebel.

17

The Minister of Consolation was getting out of his limousine when Wilson Iyari arrived at the Ministry. He had not seen Chini for a fortnight since their return and he was anxious to catch even a fleeting glimpse of her. In the manner of the Independence monuments the Ministry was a building shaped like two enormous matchboxes, one lying flat, the other on its edge on top of it. The Italian engineers claimed it was a great achievement. No one could see the water on which the building floated, but it was widely claimed that it stood on rafts and represented the first step towards creating a West African Venice out of Lagos.

At first Wilson did not quite believe his eyes, but when he looked again he found that indeed the face of the Minister had lost its handsomeness. Instead it was swathed in bandages, and so was his head.

Wilson bowed in greeting, but the Minister apparently did not see him and quickly climbed the steps into the Ministry, followed by one hundred people waving letters, singing his praises and putting bottles of beer to their lips. These were the hangers-on who brought up his tail. Wilson felt a wave of pity. No Minister was allowed to travel without his satellites or to eat without them, or even sleep. They hung on like leeches, shameless, always demanding.

Shortly after the Minister's tail had passed, Wilson saw a small car squeeze itself close to the Minister's, and Chini jumped out. Wilson moved forward instinctively.

'How're you, Willy? I've not seen you for so long.' She stretched out her hand and the little boy took it and leapt down. He wore school uniform and carried a pot of ink. 'This is my son, Babatunde.'

'The very image,' Wilson smiled. 'Francis Garret must have been proud of him.'

Now that they were back in Lagos they saw very little of each other, and already Wilson could feel their lives pursuing different routes. Wilson tried not to remember the hunting scene and the way it had ended.

'I saw your Minister in bandages. What happened?'

Chini put a hand to her lips. 'Wilson, you should know! After you have taken money from his rivals and beaten him up you come to ask me. Funny!' Her sarcasm startled him.

She did not stop to explain. Wilson followed her to the steps, and she said: 'Willy, I'm in a hurry and can't explain now. I was told it was an NMFAMS job.'

'But the NMFAMS? There's no more NMFAMS. . . . Wait a minute. . . .'

Chini had vanished up the stairs into the Independence monument, and Wilson stood there puzzled and intrigued by the unhelpful clues that Chini had dropped. 'NMFAMS job . . . taken money from his enemies . . .' Little wonder the Minister of Consolation had not answered his greeting. He must have imagined that Wilson was connected with his hardship. But how could it ever be an NMFAMS job if he were away at a conference? It did not make sense. He was glad he had seen Chini, and now he made straight for the pharmacy.

. . . . .

Kwame was waiting for him at the pharmacy. He appeared tense and secretive, and Wilson took him into the inner office.

'It's about your wife. I found where she lives.'

Wilson was mildly interested.

Kwame took out a cigarette and lit it. A woman came into the outer office with a child strapped to her back. She gave Wilson a prescription and he excused himself and took it to the retail shop. He handed over the tablets and the mixture personally to the woman, with directions.

He found Kwame reading the label on a new brand of blood tonic which he was still sampling.

'I thank you, Kwame, but I did not tell you I was looking for my wife, did I?'

'Now, Wilson, don't talk like that. You know, when I came from Ghana I found both of you living peacefully together. It was a good thing. I used to come to your place for sustenance, having been forced to leave my own family behind.' He drew at his cigarette. 'But now I have to go back. I must go back, and I want to leave you and your wife as I found you.'

'People change, Kwame. It is no longer possible to be what we were before the demonstration. The NMFAMS is gone, you are going back to Ghana——'

'And Yaniya is coming back to you.' He searched in his pockets. 'Here is the address. Don't mind what front she may present. You know women. She needs you— badly. Promise me you'll at least go and see her.'

'She killed my son.'

'You judge her and condemn her without a hearing. If she could only be given a chance, Wilson!' Kwame placed a hand on Wilson's shoulder. 'You have been a good friend. This is your own private life and only a friend can dare take a look in. The girl has repented, she has suffered enough, I tell you.'

He rose, and abruptly changed the subject. 'I shall miss Nigeria.'

Wilson was shocked. To him Kwame had become a permanent feature of his life. 'When do you leave?'

'This evening. I wanted to leave before you returned from Dakar, so as to spare you the pain. But I felt so bad about Yaniya. Now I've done my duty as a friend. . . .'

'Thank you, indeed. Kwame, would you mind if I ran you out to the border?'

'Most obliged, Wilson.'

Wilson looked him squarely in the face and said, 'How do you feel about going back?'

'Man, it's the call of home. Who can ignore that? The worst that can happen, they'll put me in detention. But, at least, my wife will know I am not on voluntary exile.'

'What about your enemies, I mean the political ones who don't want to see you alive?'

'God will protect me.' Kwame grew serious. 'Really, Wilson, the priest is giving me a special service, and that's one of the reasons why I am here. I want you to come.'

Throughout the service Kwame never once took his eyes off the altar. His lips moved incessantly, as if he were offering his soul for the last time to his Maker. He waited behind in the church, and when the priest had gone into the parish he called Wilson to accompany him. He had a proposition to put to the priest and wanted Wilson to witness it.

They found the priest standing by a flower-pot and examining the flowers.

Kwame apologized, then said, 'Priest, I have brought some money.'

'Well, that's good. But what is it for?' He took a last look at the flowers and walked over to the sitting-room where they all perched on the edges of their seats.

Wilson was amazed at the way Kwame was acting. To him it seemed portentous, but hazy.

'It's for my funeral service,' Kwame said. 'Wilson, my friend here, thinks I am going to commit suicide. But he is wrong. However, if I die . . .' He laughed uneasily. 'But I am only going home, how can I be committing suicide? I am only going home, that's all. To my country.'

'Why, young man, but you're young, and full of health. You should be thinking of life, not death.'

'I know. . . . I'm not dead yet. . . . I just have a feeling. One must be prepared to face anything. Life is fleeting.'

Wilson felt a tightness in his throat. He was like a man witnessing a blood oath. The priest took the money from Kwame.

'You are going on a journey, but your friend is here. If it makes you feel good I shall take this money and keep it for you till you return——'

'I am not returning here.'

Wilson intervened. 'Kwame, let the priest keep the money. When you need it it can still be sent to you. It's like a saving. . . .'

The priest had been counting the money. He looked up now. 'Fifty pounds, is that right?'

'Correct.'

'I'll keep it, then. And any time you want it it's yours.'

'Thank you. I feel better.' He turned to Wilson. 'Time to be setting off.'

They rose and left the parish to return to the pharmacy. On the way Kwame dropped off to complete his packing. Wilson left the car at the garage for servicing.

18

THEY drove in silence towards the last border. Kwame would soon be home. The road passed through the poorest stretch of territory, clothed in scrub and littered with abandoned farmland bare of any form of food. Peugeots, Citroens, Simcas drove past in the opposite direction, at speeds faster than the whirlwind. They were racing towards the markets in Lagos. In the morning they would be coming back heavily loaded with every edible thing from corn to salt. Their livelihood depended on entering Nigeria every day.

Wilson arrived at the Customs post and found other cars waiting. He helped Kwame with Customs formalities. Kwame stood by, hands folded, brooding. There was a girl sitting on the other side of the border, selling cigarettes, matches, a few bottles of red wine. The girl was sitting away from the table on which her wares were displayed, leaning her head against one of the posts supporting the wooden thatch hut. Her two arms were lifted above her head, her bosom arched.

Wilson saw how Kwame was staring in the direction of the girl. The top of her blouse was shifted down and she sat carelessly, apparently unaware of the yawning thighs that revealed the darker labyrinths. The roots of her breasts —sapling stems of sucklement—buried their thickness in two hefty ridges. Her bosom seemed to be divided into those two roots and nothing more, tossing up the lower edge of the blouse so that the midriff stood revealed. The skin of her breasts reflected the smile on her face.

Wilson stood beside Kwame for a few moments then muttered under his breath, 'African womanhood.' He touched Kwame. 'Let's go and buy a bottle of wine from her.'

She did not speak English but was able to sell them the bottle of wine, with shy smiles. Wilson and Kwame sat on benches and filled the glasses placed on the bare wooden tables.

They drank in silence. Kwame was so silent that Wilson became uneasy. He pushed away his glass.

'You see that girl?' Kwame said. 'She was sitting there. There, every day! She sat there until we were able to sneak across the border. I must be mad to be going back again. . . . Why, I must be a wanted man all over Ghana. That girl's eyes frighten me. She knows so much. She sits there and sells matches. She sees everything but says nothing. I am afraid of her.'

Wilson let him talk. He looked over the border at the girl. And now a stranger stood by their table. He did not order a drink, but stared fixedly at Kwame.

'Are you Kwame Amantu?' His tone and manner were insolent, sparking off Wilson's anger.

To Wilson's surprise there was no anger on Kwame's face, only fear.

'You recognize me, don't you?' Kwame asked.

'Yes, I come from the secret police.'

It was very silent on the border. The girl with the bosom was sitting quite still, with her arms clinging to the wooden support of the shed.

'You must come with me, quietly. Don't make any noise at all. They are all watching, but they do not know.'

Kwame's face changed. He now wore an insolent smile. 'If you want the reward then you must kill me. I can't come with you.'

Wilson took the cue. 'He can't come with you, Mr Secret Police.'

The gun appeared, like something out of a movie. Wilson stared unbelieving. He saw the hand, cold, steady, menacing. Kwame tensed, like a crouching leopard. In a flash he threw himself forward. There was a blast and another. The man who had fired the shots ran and twisted into a lane and in a moment his motor-cycle was speeding across the border.

In all directions men, fowls, women, goats, scurried away to safety. A Nigerian policeman leaned over Kwame Amantu, then turned him over. Kwame was dead.

At that moment Wilson looked up at the girl on the border. She had not moved, but her mouth remained open, wide enough to admit a whole orange.

To Wilson was left the task of attending Kwame's funeral service and sending his things back to his family in Ghana with condolences. When it was all over, he went down to the jail to see Brother Jacob.

Brother Jacob was in the best of spirits. Even in jail he managed to wear a shiny ruby ring on his left finger and to talk about clever devices for getting rich.

'How's my sister?'

'Yaniya, I haven't seen her.'

'I learnt she's now an air hostess. So you haven't made

up yet? Look, Wilson. Women will be women. You must go down to where she lives and make amends. She is your wife, you know.'

'Thank you.' Wilson changed the subject. 'Brother Jacob, now that Kwame is dead the NMFAMS is truly dead.'

'Kwame dead?'

The guard looked at them sharply. He seemed to have been eavesdropping.

'He died on the border. I was taking him home, and the secret police caught him. At least, the people say they are secret police. They may just have been his political enemies. He was shot before my own eyes. Terrible.'

'So sorry. He was a good man. I liked him a lot.'

'Yes. And you know why I admire him? He disagreed with his rivals but still continued to love his country. That is a great thing.'

They were silent.

Wilson looked at Brother Jacob and found his eyes full of tears. He was touched.

'You see,' Wilson said, 'I'm sure he *knew* he was going to die. Before we left for the border he took me to a priest and in my presence gave him some money. For my funeral service, he said. The priest laughed then. But you see what has happened?'

'May we all be consoled. The NMFAMS is dead but the spirit is not dead. We still want African Unity.'

Again they were silent and the atmosphere was heavy about them. Wilson looked closely at Brother Jacob and in spite of his grief he detected a certain feeling of ease.

'Brother Jacob, are you still in for the same reason?'

'No . . . I was in for the demonstration, but later released; just like yourself. I am in now for flogging

Agnes. And, again, the question of Paul Aremu. He put me inside because of his money. It is all confused.'

Wilson did not quite follow.

Brother Jacob told how he had waylaid the Minister of Consolation at a party gathering. He had then beaten him up, but the Minister of Consolation had his own thugs and in the scuffle he had escaped with injuries. This was not what Brother Jacob had expected, and when he told Paul Aremu, that wealthy man was very angry. The arrangement was that he should get rid of the Minister of Consolation.

Brother Jacob said: 'I am glad we only beat him up. I don't care what Paul Aremu may say. He has not proof that I took his money.'

'What?' Wilson asked in surprise. 'How much?'

'Five thou.'

'And where is it?'

'I used it to pay my debts.'

'You are always in debt, Brother Jacob. But this is very serious. You know how desperate Paul Aremu can be if he does not get his money. I must do something about this. I must do something. . . .'

Brother Jacob laughed. 'I hope you know that Paul Aremu thinks the NMFAMS was responsible for taking his money. I was acting on behalf of the NMFAMS. So watch out, your life is not safe.'

Wilson looked Brother Jacob over squarely. The smile of triumph angered him. 'Did you consult me or the late Kwame before you took the money—and spent it?'

'I could not find you.'

Wilson was confused. 'What does all this mean?'

'Well, in-law, you know a man like Paul Aremu does not joke with his money. And, again, he is not very happy to see that the Minister of Consolation is still alive. Personally, as I said, I am very glad. It is a big joke!' He laughed.

Wilson Iyari snapped at him. 'You shouldn't have had anything to do with him. You were there when I turned him back that day after the demonstration. Then you went behind my back. You are my in-law and your main job is to get me into trouble!' He paced about impatiently.

Now he remembered what Chini had told him outside the Ministry of Consolation. She had said something about Wilson taking money, about an NMFAMS job. ... It was clear now. Brother Jacob had implicated him, and he must extricate himself—publicly.

19

WILSON at last summoned up enough courage to call on his wife. A little girl met him at the back of the house and told him that she had 'travelled'. He did not follow what this meant, so he called at the airport, where one of the girls told him that Yaniya's plane had left for Dakar but would be back within the week.

It was evening when he called again. She was sitting on the floor, while a bare-bosomed woman was plaiting her hair. As soon as she saw him, she rose. On the rungs of the bed he saw her beret and uniform, pressed and ready for the next day at the airport.

He looked at her for a long time.

'Wilson, was it you who called?'

'Yes, I was told you were in Dakar.'

'Come into the house, please.'

He went in. The room was small, strange, and, when he thought of the men who must come here to speak to his wife, repellent.

'Your brother is in jail for beating Agnes. You know that, I hope. And you know about Paul Aremu.'

'Yes. I went to see him. . . .'

Wilson studied her in silence. He did not feel any warmth towards her, only duty. He thought of the two remaining children, Pandhit and Jomo.

'According to him, he took money from Paul Aremu in the name of the NMFAMS. Now the money is spent. And Paul Aremu wants either his money or the life of the Minister of Consolation. I am not prepared to commit murder. I drove Paul Aremu away when he came to see me. Your brother was there.'

'Won't you sit down?' said Yaniya, motioning round the room. The woman plaiting her hair tied a wrapper over her breasts and wiggled out of the room.

Wilson looked at his wife with a mixture of anger and pity. The unmentionable subject stood between them. Suddenly he saw again the Forest of Emorwen, heard the old man's voice. She seemed to sense what he was thinking.

'No . . . not murder.' Her eyes widened. 'Wilson, I did not murder . . . anyone. I am very sorry for what happened. It has made me very wretched. . . .'

'Pack your things and come back, Yaniya. You are forgiven.'

'I am useless to you now, Wilson. You know what the doctor said. And I know how you loved our Lum.'

'Pack your things and come, that's all.'

'Give me time to think.'

'There's nothing to think about. Tell your employers. Then go to Benin, or wherever the children are, and bring them back home. It is not fair to them.'

'Are you sure you still want me after what I did?'

'Of course. The NMFAMS was one of those forces that kept us apart. Now it is dissolved. I am going back to my pharmacy. And, again, you now have your work. You can be as glamorous as you like and no one will complain.'

He saw the hardness in her eyes. She turned away. 'You will promise to treat me well?'

'Haven't I been treating you well?'

'No woman likes to be neglected. You never stay at home. You leave in the morning and return late and then they come to a meeting in the house. You neglected me.' She looked underfed, wretched. She had the male-hunt look already in her eye, the mark of the single woman. Her unhappiness was being overlaid by a core of hardness.

'You will come?'

'I cannot give an answer now, Wilson. Truly, I feel confused. I cannot.'

'Don't take too long. Kwame made me promise, before he died, that we must come together. It was I who took him to the border on his way home before he met his death. I am sure there was something about him we never knew. He hid it so well from all of us. I think he *knew* his fate was sealed even before he left. Yet he went and got killed.'

'You too must be careful, Wilson. I have heard it said that Paul Aremu is after you.'

'I have done him no wrong.'

'They say he has boasted in town that he will kill you, leader of the NMFAMS.'

'That will not frighten me. I am due to give a public statement tomorrow about the NMFAMS.'

'I beg you, don't appear in public, at least for some time. Please don't.'

Wilson smiled and took his leave of Yaniya. He walked down the steps, his mind a little lighter than when he went to see his wife.

The attendance at the mass meeting staggered Wilson and long before he drove into the square there was already impatience. Wilson was taken aback at first, but he remembered that the papers had played up the NMFAMS affair. There was a particularly vicious attack in the *West African Revolution*.

He mounted the rostrum with a new feeling of maturity and soberness. When he spoke it was not in the old rabble-rousing manner he had adopted before the demonstration.

'The NMFAMS is dead, ladies and gentlemen. But its spirit continues. It must remain alive. The society was formed at a time when we as a group felt that African Unity was urgent and pressing, but its achievement has been proved to be more than complex. It requires time, it requires patience, it requires tact. We Africans are all very sensitive. We are all very proud. We are all absolutely correct in our different ways of thinking. So what is the result? Each man occupies his own invulnerable position and will remain there. What can you do but let him be or ask him to relinquish his position or for ever be his enemy?

'Gentlemen and ladies, I am bowing out of the NMFAMS as a movement. We have achieved our desires. This country is already on the path to uniting all other African countries. The leaders are human and must make mistakes, but they are following the right path.'

He stepped down and sat on the long table, waiting for questions. Looking back on it all, Wilson did not quite know why he called this meeting. But it was on, and he must see it through. At least it would serve to show the people what they wanted to know about the present stand of the NMFAMS.

He looked up and saw that the crowd was making

way for a young woman who pushed her way through them. It was his wife, Yaniya. She had come out in public to sit by him. He felt pleased.

'Wilson, I cancelled my flight just to be here on this last day of the NMFAMS. I was so worried.'

'I am grateful.' No longer did he feel alone now.

In the distance Wilson saw a black Cadillac looking for parking space. He was listening to the question being asked with half an ear. His breath stuck. Sweat appeared on his wrists and he brought out his handkerchief and wiped them.

The man who came out of the Cadillac looked to him from that distance like Paul Aremu, but he could not really tell. The significance of his presence did not immediately dawn on Wilson, but when he saw three men jump down and mingle with the crowd he turned and noticed that Yaniya too had been observing them.

'I warned you, Wilson. They have come to cause confusion.'

Wilson bit his lip. He could not break up the meeting now. There would be no explanation. He was answering questions mechanically. A man with a dark beard appeared before the table opposite Wilson and spoke. Someone asked a question from the back and the bearded man turned and shouted at him.

Yaniya held Wilson by the arm. 'Be cool. They have been paid to cause confusion. Be cool. . . .'

The two strangers hurled abuse at each other. Confusion threatened the assembly. On the edge of the crowd Wilson saw the riot police tumbling out of a truck, armed with batons and shields. He searched for Paul Aremu's Cadillac and found that it was no longer parked there. It seemed at first that the confusion would die down, but suddenly it flared up. Attention was diverted from the rostrum.

Suddenly a man took three steps towards Wilson and raised his arm. A knife blade flashed. In that split-second Yaniya threw herself across Wilson, intercepting the blow.

She clung to him and groaned. The thug melted into the crowd. The crowd broke up into groups being herded away by the police.

Wilson was leaning over Yaniya, in tears. 'You saved my life, Y. Why did you do it?'

She said nothing. The pain showed in her eyes, in her gritted teeth.

'Are you seriously hurt, Y.?'

'It's nothing, really. Has the ambulance come?'

'It's there. The police are here too.'

'I'm glad, Willy. I feel very happy, especially for Lum. . . . He is avenged.'

'You must live, you must not die.' He broke out into a loud sob, calling her by name, praying to God to save her.

'It is good like this, I am so happy. . . . Wilson, I am no use to you any longer. I told you. See that girl, Chini? She's for you. She loves you, really. I've known it all along. She'll look after Pandhit and Jomo very well. With her, I have no fear. . . . Take care of her. She worships you. Did you know that?'

'What are you talking about, Y.? You know you must live, you must not die.'

'You need her. You need Chini, to build again. Go back to the pharmacy. Leave all this business . . . leave the leaders to do their leading. . . .' Her eyes had a strange glow.

The stretcher-bearers laid the stretcher beside her and lifted her on to it. Wilson followed them to see that she was comfortable in the ambulance.

He was leaving the parade-ground when he saw a small car arrive. It was Chini who got out of it, and with her were two children.

When they came nearer Wilson saw that Pandhit was there and also Jomo.

'A surprise for you, Wilson. Yaniya told me to send for them. She's gone to Dakar, you know.'

Wilson was in tears. 'Thank you, Chini. Bless you. Do you see the ambulance . . . your friend is inside.'

'What happened?'

'They stabbed her. It was me they wanted and she saved my life. I am going at once to the hospital. Will you come?'

'Yes,' said Chini, and they set off.

Wilson found that the events of the last few months had established him as a national figure. When he sat in the INDEPENDENCE PHARMACY and breathed the familiar aroma of balsams and antiseptics he felt at ease. He found also that more people made their way to the shop. He wanted to imagine that they came because he was a good pharmacist (which he was) but he could not dismiss the idea that his part in recent events awakened the curiosity of a good many of them and they came to meet him. And so he obliged them with long stories in between one sale and the other, or while waiting for a prescription to be dispensed.

Whenever evening came round and he saw the *Bole-kaja* (get down, let's fight) lorries unloading their passengers in front of the INDEPENDENCE PHARMACY he thought of that long-postponed visit to the Lagos Town Council. One day he would make it and the bus stop would be shifted.

His first patient this evening was a woman who came in and in her roundabout manner laid a long complaint which Wilson could not understand. He referred her to a doctor.

When she slipped out a girl slipped in.

'Chini!'

'I've been waiting in the shop. . . .' She looked radiant. 'I am so happy the worst is over for your wife . . .'

'Bless her.'

'I have Pandhit and Jomo with me, in the car, but we will not disturb you. . . . Glad you're back in pharmacy. No more dabbling in politics. I must go now. I'll take them home till Yaniya can look after them.'

'Thank you, Chini. I'll come and see them.'

He choked back a sob. Now she could be a friend of the family, openly so because her conscience was clear. He watched her, trim and smart as always, and so selfless.

The children were seated at the back of the car and when they saw Wilson they cried, 'Papa!' and it was enough satisfaction for him that they remembered and recognized him even in the poor light.

20

He visited the hospital daily. The nurses knew him and allowed him to overstay his time to help Yaniya in all she wanted. Chini cooked delicious meals and nursed the children. She drove them to the hospital in her car and kept out of sight when they visited their mother.

In their long moments together Yaniya thawed. Gradually, she bared her heart to Wilson. She still loved him, but frustration and loneliness had been driving her outside, into arms that held neither security nor satisfaction. She had discovered that men liked married women to stay married. In this way husbands would take the responsibilities and they as lovers would take only the pleasures. She told Wilson of Gadson Salifas, her lover when she had been protected by Wilson, but when alone and in need he had turned his back on her, refusing to help her.

Wilson told her of his own search for a home outside when she left him. But it never satisfied. Marriage was something more rounded than mere infatuation, and once a man had built his home, things were different with him. He must still need his home and would never be the same without it. He had found Chini, had desired her, only to find he could not take her, she was so sisterly and good-natured. It appeared they were all set for a new life.

Daily he drove home, and now the children were back with him. Chini had left for the United Nations where she would work as secretary-typist for eighteen months.

One evening, when Wilson called, Yaniya had been sitting waiting for some time.

'I'm discharged,' she said, on seeing the surprise on his face.

He was happy.

Brother Jacob had been released, and he and Agnes, Wilson and the children all trooped to the hospital to welcome her home. It was the festival season and they killed a ram and made a big feast. Palm fronds had been staked into the ground to form a shelter and all the girls at the airport had come. From Geneva a postcard arrived from Chini talking of peace and the great mountains of Switzerland.

They drank, they feasted into the middle of the night and a band played. Wilson was touched by the new attitude of Yaniya. He could not believe his eyes or his ears. They had truly come together now. It could be said of him that he was famous outside and that at home he had the backing of a family united by bonds of love. Wilson's beautiful feathers had ceased to be superficial and had become a substantial asset.